Fast Forward

Copyright © 2012 by FF>> Press

All rights reserved. Except for brief passages quoted in newspaper, magazine, radio or television review, no part of this publication may be published, reproduced, performed, distributed, or transmitted in any forms of media, or by any other means electronic or mechanical including photocopy, recording or any information storage and retrieval system now known or to be invented, without permission in writing from the authors, their authorized agents or heirs.

Published by FF>> Press.

ISBN: 978-0-9817852-8-8

Library of Congress Control Number: 2012948753

cover design: Nancy Stohlman
cover art: Susan Ryplewski
typesetting/layout design: M.D'Alessandro

Fast Forward

a collection of flash fiction
Volume 5

edited by
  Leah Rogin-Roper
  Stacy Walsh
  & Dustin Dill

FF>> Press 2012

Contents

Introduction   **i**

Short Shorts

The Bride *>> Robin Hawke*	**1**
My Life with Animals *>> Maureen Traverse*	**2**
The End *>> Rachel Blomstrom*	**3**
Sometimes the Only Response is Silence *>> Travis Cebula*	**4**
What We Bury, What We Don't *>> Len Kuntz*	**5**
Imitation of Life *>> Thomas Kearnes*	**7**
Two Full Minutes *>> Dan Kilkelly*	**8**
First Date *>> Nick Busheff*	**9**

Prompts
Freaks, Dreams, Science Fiction and Surrealism

The Syndicate *>> Christopher Linforth*	**12**
The Monstrosity *>> Drew Hetzel*	**16**
Inherited Tastes *>> Teresa Milbrodt*	**19**
Acts of Faith *>> Andrew Touhy*	**22**
Somnium of Posterus Somnium *>> S.C. Townsley*	**24**
Three Visitors *>> Chris Ransick*	**27**
Last of the Three Ravens *>> Erin Virgil*	**31**

On the Experience of Rain >> Bede Moloney	**33**
The Last Velociraptor >> Bernard O'Rourke	**37**
What's Strange >> Paul Corman-Roberts	**39**
The Detritus >> Nancy Stohlman	**41**

Prompts
History and [Pop] Culture

I'm Pretty Sure Nicolas Cage	
is My Gynecologist >> Kona Morris	**46**
In it to Win >> Robert Vaughan	**49**
The Final Frontier >> Phil Reece	**52**
Touchdown Jesus >> Adam Hofbauer	**54**
Virgin Debacle >> Meg Tuite	**56**
Ball, Shark, Pool, and C-3PO >> Jon Olsen	**60**

Prompts
Hybrids and Hermaphrodites

Distillation >> Sacha Siskonen	**65**
The Rod of Correction >> Nate Jordon	**68**
A Trip to the Store >> Roberta Hartling Gates	**71**
He Broke Pictures >> Carolyn Zaikowski	**75**
45-Year Rain >> Kathryn Winograd	**77**
Tent >> JP Vallières	**79**

Prompts
Science, Nature and Place

Cold Feet >> Bryan Jansing	**86**
Welcome Wharf >> Jennifer Springsteen	**89**
Guide to Dissecting the First	
Bird of Spring >> John Sibley Williams	**92**
Pathetic Fallacy >> Susan Lewis	**94**
Isn't That True? >> Sonja Larsen	**95**
Grid-Lock >> Lucy Black	**97**
Centerville >> Donna Laemmlen	**100**
Feeding the Birds >> Kirby Wright	**103**
Burning Out >> Matthew Purdy	**105**

Prompts
Characters

Tattoos >> John Paul Jaramillo	**112**
Last Cuts >> Andy Bailey	**116**
In the Leaves >> Emma Gilbert	**120**

Not Like You, Not At All >> Venita Blackburn	**122**
Readiness >> Lee Reilly	**123**
Candy Cane >> Shari Hack Jones	**126**
Her Favorite Color >> Christopher Duggan	**128**
Unable to Wrap Neat Packages >> Myra King	**130**
Stillman >> Amy Braziller	**133**
Wanting >> Brian Alan Ellis	**136**
The Ambulance Driver >> Nicholas Morris	**138**

Prompts
Sins, Secrets, Confessions and Obsessions

I Caught my Daughter's Hair	
on Fire Today >> Jamey Trotter	**141**
Covet the Compulsion >> Richard Hartwell	**145**
How Temperance Made a Decision >> Evon Davis	**147**
Knackers >> Mark Fallon	**148**
Voyeur >> Terry Persun	**152**
Purpose >> Amber Gordon	**154**
Greeting from Tel Aviv >> Jonathan Danielson	**157**
Not Stealing Raymond Carver >> John Kuebler	**160**
Three Things I Never Did after	**162**
that Summer >> Shelby Yaffe	

Prompts
Index

Introduction

flash fiction: a spy in the house of pedagogy

In preparation for Chicago's 2012 Association of Writers and Writing Programs (AWP) panel, "Flash Fiction: How and Why to Teach It," the panelists shared tiny expensive donuts and hotel coffee while we debated whether flash fiction deserved its own college course. We uncovered that what is actually happening is that teachers all over the country, and perhaps the world, are already teaching flash fiction in introductory creative writing courses. Whether or not administratively-approved flash fiction courses are accessible for undergraduates, flash fiction is sneaking in under classroom doors and creeping in through poorly sealed textbooks to become a secret agent in the creative writing teacher's cache.

Its infiltration of basic creative writing courses makes sense: flash fiction is engaging, perfect for the limited time frame of in-class critiques, and encourages experimentation and revision. There is also an area of flash fiction that bridges poetry and prose, an intersection where students who are just learning how to write creatively can focus on the relationship between precise language and storytelling. Flash fiction is the most democratic of all writing forms. Even my developmental writing students, most of whom have battled against the confines of language for their literate lives, get inspired when we write six-word stories. Suddenly students who never thought that writing could be fun have big grins on their faces while they argue over the exact connation of a word.

Flash 101: Surviving the Fiction Apocalypse is designed to not only be enjoyed for the diversity and quality of its writing, as any of Fast Forward's anthologies, but it is also designed as a resource to inspire writing. Whether you are a writer, a teacher, or just a lover of literature, I encourage readers to use this book to better understand flash fiction and to create your own.

This book is organized into seven sections. **Short-Shorts** are very short stories, some as short as six words and all under 200 words. **Freaks, Dreams, Science Fiction, and Surrealism** includes a wide range of stories that depend on a loose view of reality. **History and (Pop) Culture** are stories that base themselves in cultural references. **Hybrids and Hermaphrodites** explores experiments with form. **Science, Nature, and Place** contains stories that explore our interconnected environment. **Characters,** perhaps the most standard prose category, is made up of stories that are fueled by strong characters. **Sins, Secrets, Confessions, and Obsessions** are stories

Introduction

that examine the more perverse side of humanity. As in any attempt to classify, there are pieces that defy categorization, but my hope is that the way I've grouped these stories together makes them easier, not just to read, but to use. If you are looking for a specific story, you can also use the index to look it up by the author's last name.

Another way this book is useful for writers, teachers, and readers is through the inclusion of writing prompts connected to each section. If you're anything like me, you might read something and wish you had written it first. All good writers know they are also thieves, or at least borrowers working within a tradition. The prompts are intended to be thought-provoking for writers as well as anyone who wants to look more deeply at how flash fiction functions. While every piece in this book is not attached to an exercise, they are all stories that I find moving in a selfish "damn, I want to write like that!" kind of way. I hope you are as inspired as I am by Fast Forward's fifth anthology of flash fiction.

—Leah Rogin-Roper, May 15, 2012

Short Shorts

When teaching Hemingway's legendary "For sale: baby shoes, never used" six-word piece to a class of fifth graders, I was amazed at all the inferences they came up with: the mom is a shopaholic; the baby was born with giant feet; the ad is part of some international shoe-smuggling ring. The standard adult reading of this story is very different than the possibilities it opens for an imaginative fifth grader. Short-shorts are also very helpful for teachers to use when trying to get students to see the benefit of working within a form. Just as Robert Frost famously compared writing non-metered poetry to "playing tennis with the net down," writing exactly six words or 100 words forces writers to pay very careful attention to their diction—words not included are just as important as those that are. In this section notice the deliberate use of language, distilled.

The Bride
Robin Hawke

The bride kept dancing with Steve.

My Life with Animals
Maureen Traverse

When I was five, our dog died because my father wouldn't take her to the vet. "Animals aren't people," he told our next-door neighbor. A day later the man next door gave me a wiggly mutt. In the garage, the man and I rubbed its belly.

"It's a boy," the man said.

"How do you know?" I asked.

He undid his belt and showed me the difference.

No one could ever train that dog. It dug up all the plastic soldiers I buried in the yard. You could yell, but it would just stand there panting, waving that tail like a flag.

The End
Rachel Blomstrom

"Wipe that look out of your eyes," she said to no one. Desolation. Charred wood smoldered before her. Heat ran through her worn soul.

"Go west," they said. "Head for the coast," they said.

It's not all gone. She believed it. She breathed it. She ate hope.

Now, ice cold wind whipped her hair and stung her dirty cheeks. Sand flew in her eyes. The ground burned her feet and knees. To her left was a black ocean; and to her right, as far as she knew, was the fire at the end of the world.

Sometimes the Only Response is Silence
Travis Cebula

He pulled a draft of wine nearly as black as his jacket.
"Invented graffiti," he said.
"What?"
"Graffiti. I invented it. 1971."

What We Bury, What We Don't

Len Kuntz

Past midnight, I wake to find she's gone.

My wife's not soaking in the tub, as she is so often lately. She's not in the kitchen either. In fact, every room is empty, even Lonnie's.

I finally find her in the backyard on her knees, digging with bare hands, a lantern lying lopsided to help her see. Showers of dirt whisk over the arc of light and then are swept invisible by darkness. No crickets bleat. The street is dead, too. Only the wall-eyed moon looks on warily.

"Honey," I say.

Her hand springs up. A stop sign. A warning that is no longer new.

It's November, cold, the earth packed hard. It takes my wife over an hour. She brings the thing out of the soil as if it were our dead child instead of little Lonnie's killer, my old pistol.

While she weeps, the moon respectfully turns its back behind a cloud quilt. My wife staggers to her feet, a jumble of bones and dermis, like the day of the accident.

She hands me the pistol, snout-end out. "I want you to burn it. Melt it down to nothing," she says. "Then I want you gone for good."

Imitation of Life
Thomas Kearnes

I still have the fake yellow rose you bought me. It was cheap and awful. You presented it from the doorway our first weekend together. You apologized for it. The rose was wrapped in clear plastic. Underneath, imitation lace wound around the stem. It's nothing, you said. I kissed you as the door stood open. Any neighbor might happen upon two young men kissing on my front porch. You were often more inhibited. The ferocity of my emotions disturbed you. Four years later, your fake rose stays pinned to my wall.

I've let many men inside my home since you slammed my door that final time, but none have asked about it. If one does, I will tell him this story. I will tell him it's my first flower from a boy. I will tell him it is not real, so it cannot die.

Two Full Minutes
Dan Kilkelly

For two full minutes, the assistant was taken by her superior in the broom closet. It was just commonplace enough for her to snicker afterwards.

First Date
Nick Busheff

At the opera, she chugged beer.

Prompts

1. Using "The Bride" and "First Date" as models, write the story of a relationship in six words.

2. Write your own life story in six words.

3. In exactly 100 words, tell a story about a childhood pet, as in "My Life With Animals."

4. "The End," was inspired by Cormac McCarthy's *The Road*. Write a condensed version of your own favorite literary masterpiece in 200 words or less.

5. In under 100 words, write a story that is mostly dialogue, as in "Sometimes the Only Response is Silence."

Freaks, Dreams, Science Fiction and Surrealism

The resurgence of flash fiction is an international phenomenon, partially because it functions as an ideal form for magical realism and other surrealist styles. The form of flash fiction is often spurred by a suspension of disbelief, wherein the reader accepts that the writer will not be providing them with every detail. In a flash fiction piece, it is often enough to have an aspect of the surreal play out in a realistic setting, while other pieces invent an entire dream world. Characters can change forms, self-cannibalize, and startling imagery can kindle an entire piece. This section is a celebration of the fantastical in flash fiction.

The Syndicate
Christopher Linforth

One Tuesday, last month, after an audition for Shakespeare's *As You Like It*, and after a coffee with a fellow rejected actor, the Syndicate emailed my agent a proposition: Wanted—*Professional Applause Man*. When I started out, I'd heard of this shadowy organization, but thought little of the bizarre rumors that surrounded it. So I was intrigued, a day later, when an envelope reached my apartment in Williamsburg. The letter contained a list of rules to govern my behavior. It rambled on for a while about appropriate attire: a tuxedo for the opera, slacks and a button down shirt for a musical, faded skinny jeans and a plaid shirt for an art house play. When it reached my role, it noted there would be no one-handed clapping or jovial slapping of the leg. The letter mentioned that I must clap both palms together in an even one-one pattern, showing only a modicum of enthusiasm.

Before I could sign and return the contract, I needed to agree to the confidentiality clause. No friends or family could know of my employment. At first, I considered that it was a prank, a set-up by my agent, or a practical joke planned by a slighted ex-lover. I had little choice, though: acting gigs had run dry and I hadn't lowered myself to passing out discount shoe flyers or delivering Chinese restaurant menus.

A week after mailing in my acceptance, I received my first call. A distorted voice told me the details: "*The Bagel Wars*, Ridgemont Theater, 8 p.m. Make it look good." I'd been to the Ridgemont a year back for an audition. The place was a converted garment factory, remodeled with a proscenium arch and stage, and two hundred thinly cushioned seats. On arriving, the line outside was sparse. A handful of foreign tourists in slacks and matching blue windbreakers smiled politely at the manager, who offered them quarter-price tickets in his butchered high school German.

At the booth I gave the "Lox" codeword the voice had supplied. The attendant passed through a ticket for third row center. Inside the theater, I took my seat. A few other patrons were situated at the rear. For ninety minutes I watched in horror. The play focused on two East Village bagel stores in the 1920s. One was trying to undercut the other by cutting out the boiling stage of the process and so producing cheaper bagels that were inferior in taste and quality. It seemed to be a critique of post-war capitalism; however, the performances were inscrutably bad. The lead was an Englishman making his debut. He displayed an annoying habit of mixing up a Queens accent with a Southern drawl and calling for missed lines from the stage manager.

At the end of the performance, I was the first to clap. I started slow at first, a kind of unintentional mocking pulse. By luck the other patrons didn't notice me until I stood. In an attempt to undo my first weak effort, I clapped in long, booming strokes and gave forth the occasional, but genuine sounding, "Encore!" The rest of the audience already had their coats on, and were halfway out of the aisle, when they stopped and looked at me, and then the cast, who were giving their second bow. Behind me came a smatter of polite clapping. One man even said he'd pay to watch the show again, though he seemed to be trying to impress the redhead hanging on his shoulder.

Back at my apartment, I wasn't sure if I'd hear again from the Syndicate. But, a few days later, a call came for another job and then a third. The hefty paychecks made up for the sore, callused hands and the tubes of medicinal salves I bought to soothe them. After attending a half-dozen shows, it occurred to me that I was attending a collection of sub-par productions: remixed Shakespeare, post-apocalyptic Pinter, musicals featuring lewd sock puppets, and a six-hour existential hurrah on painters that never painted. Most shows were off-Broadway and it appeared to suggest the Syndicate consisted of theater owners, producers, and maybe even writers. It seemed that I was there to encourage the actors as much as the audience. On stage they looked to the exit in hope of an escape, as though they were trapped in the awfulness of their roles.

Over the weeks my technique-of-the-hand—as it became known—progressed to a more nuanced level. My applause contained intricate patterns of syncopation, often building to multiple crescendos in a fast-slow-fast rhythm. Some people compared it to Mozart's *Paris Symphony*. I even heard rumors that audiences across Broadway had caught on to the trend and that other Applause Men had copied my style.

During a production of *Tally-ho!*, a fox hunting tragedy set in stuffy 1930s Britain, my efforts fell flat. In the matinee performances I was often the only audience member. I sat in the stalls, always looking back to the entrance to see if other patrons would join me. Few ever came through the doors. Watching the show, every day, I soon learnt the lines by rote and a rapport grew between the actors and me. Sometimes they rotated their acting to where I was sitting. Other times they said their lines to the rear of the stage, laughing under their breath. Then one morning the lead called in sick and the stand-in refused to go on, citing the death of his career if he stepped upon those boards. Without anyone asking, I took to the stage. In unison, the actors doffed their black riding helmets and then cracked their crops on their starched breeches. That night, I inhabited the Master of Fox Hounds role and during the final monologue—where I confessed to the murder of a young kennel-man—I showed the Syndicate I could act. That I was someone. After my speech was over, I stepped forward and looked at the darkened stalls, clasped my hands together behind my back, and waited.

The Monstrosity
Drew Hetzel

"Hold it where I can see it," Clarisse says. She's no doubt eyeing his Monstrosity, "and stop moving it around."

They're at it again in their trailer as I'm gargling and oiling my sword for the afternoon show. I've seen them at it a dozen times.

"I'm not moving it," Frank says, resigned and sorrowful.

He clearly doesn't like it when she tells him what to do, but the way I've seen her look at him after she looks at it, well.

"I never get to see it. Wait! God, it's so floppity. Is it moving on its own?"

She's probably cocking her head in this silence, trying to take it all in.

"Okay, I'm putting it away now."

"Wait!"

She reaches for it—he pushes her arm away.

"Don't touch it!"

"Oh… it's so… unique."

He handles it with both hands as he tries to put it back in.

"Can't I touch it?"

"Why?"

"Because it's so different, that's all. I don't mind."

"Why the hell would you mind?"

"That's not what I mean. Here, I just want to pet it."

"It's not a pet."

"I didn't say it was a pet, I said I want to pet it, pet it."

"No."

He finally pushes it down and tucks it in as if he'd been waiting for it to go back on its own.

Before the circus it was just a play-toy, something to scare the girls or get a laugh from his friends when they got drunk. Now it's all he has. It looks fragile, but it got caught in the towel rack, got sat on, even got slammed in a car door once, and nothing ever happens to it. The sheer girth of the thing, the creases and folds, so many places for a mold or a fungus. If it gets infected and has to be cut off, he'll be out of a job. He cleans it every night with alcohol and calamine lotion. He cleans it even when Clarisse won't leave.

Clarisse. He thinks he loves her, but things are never clear in the circus—everything changes. He wonders if she fancies him just for his Talent, and has to admit that he fancies her for her third nipple and the Talent she shows the customers, her pig tail that sticks out of a hole in her pink suede pants lined with hot pink fur.

She tells me and Frank over a beer that she feels

pacified every time she sees The Monstrosity. The audacity of the thing makes her feel calm, "If there's room for The Monstrosity in this world, there's room for all us sinners!" she says like a southern preacher. He knows she's just trying to get a rise out of him, but it makes him feel like a freak when he hears her say that, and even though he is a freak, he doesn't want to hear it from her. Anyhow, with her interest in The Monstrosity, and his interest in her interest, they have a thing. It must feel like something solid.

Inherited Tastes
Teresa Milbrodt

You know everyone has vaguely carnivorous aunts who threaten small children with consumption—You're so cute I could just eat you up—then they laugh it off like a joke, a figure of speech, too quick to search for deeper meanings. Old ladies may not pose that danger, but eating yourself is a product of too-human narcissism, secret desire, imagining your taste must be fantastic, and this is why it's dangerous to start nibbling on a finger.

Especially in your family.

Your aunts and uncles and cousins all assume their own sweet flesh is superior, and that's the only thing that keeps you from devouring each other. It maintains an odd harmony among your clan of self-cannibals as you sit around the table after Thanksgiving dinner, stuffed with turkey and cranberries and sweet potatoes, fighting the urge to nip tiny bites from the inside of your wrist as you commiserate about the habit no one is able to break.

Your uncle has done research, tried to find out if other family lines have been stricken with an eating disorder like this, but if such is the case they must have kept it well hidden. No historical records exist, not that you'd blame them for silence. You're all sick of trying to explain the disease to doctors, since the medical community has been of no help.

At every holiday gathering or reunion, myths circulate about what remained of this or that long-dead relative when they finally passed on. Your great-aunt Hilde's casket was regular-sized, but that was just for show. No one recalls how much of her was buried. Everyone wants to maintain healthy public appearances, so you're all good at feigning normality. Your Uncle Stanley, who works as an accountant and is missing both pinkies and all his toes, says there could be worse afflictions, but he can't think of any when pressed.

The process of consumption is pleasant, but the remorse after eating your arm to the elbow...that's a real level of hell. Your Uncle Roger tells everyone he's a war vet when asked to explain his two prosthetic legs, a good tactic since the questioners nod solemnly and don't press further. Roger couldn't disclose how he gets hungry late at night and, well, things happen. His daughter, your cousin Mallory, was caught in the girl's room at school munching near her shoulder, something easily hidden by a sleeve. It was a long and sorrowful fight to keep her out of an institution, but now that she's being home-schooled by your aunt, things are much happier. Your aunt just has to make sure Mallory has a steady supply of licorice so she avoids chewing on other things, but she's been snacking on her tongue in the middle of algebra lessons.

The threat is enough to make you keep your own supply of licorice at the ready, warding off the inevitable. If you eat yourself down to the bone, all that's left is your lonely and contented head, rolling around like an aimless soccer ball with a smug smile. You were indeed delicious, a once-in-a-lifetime experience. After that you can nibble on your hair, something that will regenerate, just don't bite your lips because then, surely, all is lost.

Acts of Faith
Andrew Touhy

I woke to the bright round moon crowding our window, shining down on a final tiny acrobat steadying himself soundlessly on a tightrope strung from my heart to yours while we slept. There was, it seemed, an entire army of them: slippered and poised, all dressed in green tights and short capes, their taut arms folded in muscular defiance. "Jesus what are you doing here?" I said, trying to hold my voice to a whisper. "Go away now. You'll wake her." And out came the cannonballs. Out came the bowling pins and spinning dinner plates. Out came the handkerchiefs and chainsaws, the juggling knives and glowing torches, the hoops, umbrellas, and ladders, the wheelbarrows and pets and very small children. It was a nightmare: a great noisy cloud of maneuvers and props whirled tirelessly between us, threatening to come raining down, threatening to send you crashing from a dream. "Guys," I said through clenched teeth, sitting up some though careful not to sway or shake them loose. "Back to the circus now, or wherever you're from, okay? She's sleeping." Your eyelids twitched at these words and you rolled closer. I backed off but reached to wipe a bit of night drool from the pinches of your soft mouth. They tossed everything higher, jumped in tandem from the strained rope to such a frightening height above our bed, everything—including my breath—suspended in midair. "Don't worry," you said then, eyes suddenly open, clear. "They'll leave of their own accord. Or they're not going anywhere. Or maybe they were never really here to begin with. Just lie back and go to sleep, I promise you'll see." With that, you brushed your lips against mine and the moon disappeared. And so did you—not even the wrinkled impression of your body left on the sheet, and the rope fell away, of course, and my eyelids grew so heavy; heavy and heavier, like all those little acrobats and their tricks, each falling into my arms, one after another in the dark.

Somnium of Posterus Somnium

S.C. Townsley

Deep within a dream, deep within a starship, trademarked twin superheroes prepare to display my future to my two-year-old self. An enormous monitor fills with color—

There is a city standing tall, spread long, crossing islands and oceanic clefts with snow-packed suspension bridges. It is The One City, the place that resides in America's heartlands but sports a sign notating the mileage to Paris, France (aside the road which leads exactly there). I crouch upon dusky rooftops and learn secrets from a young orangutan. Her voice is disturbing, unnatural; it makes me sad. The sky is such an ugly orange. You die.

Lady Baby Jesus appears in a tree house after a snowstorm. There are deer tracks in the silent night. My suggestion is that we name her "Peter." You adopt a small village of tribal Africans while I'm at work. This severely complicates my plans for the evening. You die.

Gripping grass with toes and fingers, I run on all fours. Earth tilts to accommodate me; a grin of pure pleasure breaks my face apart. I stake a miniature poodle to my leg with a bowie knife, the blood becomes polygons. Slavering with senselessness, I fuck a decapitated horse's head. In a process that is both fascinating and excruciating, my penis secretes sharp plastic beads with pictures inside. This becomes a fad—everyone wants one. You die.

There is music in a colony of aspen. A coming storm is angry lavender; autumn leaves plaster the soft ground. Submerged in the roots of an ashen tree I find a tape deck; from it, speaker wires stretch up, across, and out in every direction, running to hundreds of speakers hidden among a forest of bare branches. I can't wait to tell you. You wreck the car. It's never your fault; I'm never the one at the wheel. You die.

Duty demands that I must impregnate the moon. A colossal woman grows out of the lunar surface and I strap a rocket to my celestial dick to combat an erectile malfunction. She cannot make me cum. You tell me you hate me. I cry. We move to another city—a place of sacrifice, where wild packs of tornados reduce work to rubble, where we watch with awe. Movie theatres go green by selling only green peppers at concession stands. I get a second job being a blue whale. You die.

Hawaii vacation with a large group of friends; I've never been before. You leave me alone in the hotel. Lucille Ball, telekinetic witch, tries to kill me, destroying a department store in the process. Screaming threats, she and Captain Ahab cajole me into hauling wooden barrels of chum aboard the *Pequod*. The hotel bartender serves us the surprise special of the evening: pink lemonade spewed forth from his right nostril. It's delicious. You die.

One of my childhood bed sheets hangs in an empty airplane hangar. Something about it isn't right. The Jakobi have come to kill everyone in our isolated space station. I hide, terrified in deep sublevels. I know what horrors come for us. My teeth fall out. You die.

Mom stops her fifty-five Chevy on a hill in the jungle. An albino gorilla blocks the mud road. It signs something; we don't know sign language. Wild eyed, a man bursts into the room and shoots me five times. I bleed to death. The funeral is later that day; I attend in spirit. You die, and die, and die. My world falls apart.

An asteroid collides with Earth. I wake as a survivor, hunkered beneath a mattress in the street, surrounded by body parts and rubble. A second moon hangs in the sky. The Universe is suddenly blank—nothing—dark. I am told to create my own world. Lava cools, grass grows, terrain moves with the undulation of my fingers. Merging with the world I've created, I feel a city shake, feel 2,996 people die—crying out in terror, suddenly silenced.

The monitor dims, leaving only echoes of what I've been shown.

"I don't understand," I tell the twins, slowly waking.

"That's alright," Jayna says. "You're not supposed to."

Three Visitors
Chris Ransick

He hadn't heard her come into his office.

Early May. Sun hot on the Russian Olive trees at the edge of the expansive lawn, sharp white light on dusty grey leaves, on bright green blades beneath. Moments earlier, Magnuson had come to the brink of tears, not because of what was written on the paper in front of him but because he saw the text for what it was—one swell in an ocean he'd swum through all his adult life, current pushing him back from the distant but visible coast of everything that ever mattered. But he had laughed instead, a chortle at how ridiculous that sounded. He marked a red 78 points—the paper was a weak swing at a fast pitch—and began formulating a frank written assessment in his head: *If you had tried at all, this could have been a good response to the question of theme in Carver's story. Good ideas, misshapen and random, are water without a vase.* Brief, clever, and it teaches, he thought. He moved to write it down.

The young woman cleared her throat and he

looked up, startled.

Is this a bad time?

Magnuson shook his head and gestured to the empty chair. What can I do for you, Madison?

Melissa, she said. She dropped an enormous, swollen backpack so heavily that the paper clips in Magnuson's top drawer chimed. Melissa was sweating, rather a lot, and breathing with some trouble.

My asthma, she said. It acts up in Spring. But that's not what I came to talk about.

Magnuson, with effort, looked at her openly.

I want to talk about my grades, she said. Specifically, the C you gave me on the last assignment.

Her eyes were an unusual pale green—he'd noticed it the first session. Now he connected her in his mind. She always sat in the front row at Wednesday night's class, Introduction to Humanities. She never spoke, never proposed a question or a perspective on anyone else's. The first time she did raise her hand was the week before the midterm. Magnuson had hurried to call on her, sensing a breakthrough.

Is there a study guide for the midterm exam, she had asked.

Yes, there is, he said, and picked up the textbook, holding it open to a page marked with his notes. It's called the textbook. Read it, mark it, study it, write about it in your notebook, bring questions to class or to my office hours—like I said at the first class, and often since. Do that and you'll be ready for the midterm.

She had received the rebuke fairly well, even laughed along with the rest of the class. By the time the laughter subsided, and with it the tension in the room, there she was in the front row looking vaguely upset, just as she always looked. Just as she looked right at this moment.

Except it wasn't Melissa. It was Bonnie.

Bonnie in a smart, blue pantsuit and enough makeup that Magnuson imagined he could work it like soft clay if he were only to reach out his fingers. That thought, and the realization that he'd no idea what just happened, made him fold his hands together tightly for fear he'd give in to the impulse. Bonnie had been appointed Dean several years ago, replacing a venerable and fair-minded woman who'd done the job well for two decades. She brought with her about as much practical knowledge of education as Magnuson had regarding how to pilot an F-16, which was none.

I was passing by and just wanted to stop in and see how you're doing today, she said, her voice elevated a creepy half-octave. Bonnie smiled with her lips, the rest of her face preternaturally static.

What happened to Melissa, he asked.

Excuse me, Bonnie said. Melissa who?

Never mind, Magnuson said. For no reason at all, he thought about a hike he'd taken a few weeks ago when he'd come upon a flock of twenty or so enormous Turkey Vultures in a copse of cottonwoods on the slopes of the Sangre de Cristos. Which are the females, he'd wondered.

So, she said, and folded her hands in her lap.

Magnuson thought about doing a number of things at that moment—speaking in tongues, offering her a stale cracker from his desk drawer, or just turning back to the papers on his desk. Instead, he looked her in the eye and said, I'm not sure what you want to know but let's just say the answer is yes.

Bonnie squinted at him. I didn't come here to play games, Geoff. I think we can respect each other, even if we don't like each other.

And Magnuson knew he should not say it, even as he did. It's not a matter of disliking you, he said. I just generally don't think about you.

Magnuson relaxed his hands, now going numb from the clenching, and looked past her toward the line of trees freshly hung with leaves. Everything out there was in motion, scented, flashing. He projected himself, a yogi levitating and passing through the glass, arcing down to a lush spot of grass in dappled shade.

That always was the problem, Bonnie said. Except it wasn't Bonnie now.

The voice, too familiar for him to mistake, had for so long been the last thing he heard at night and the first thing he heard in the morning. A voice that like a reverse knife had grown sharper with years of use.

That always was the problem, she repeated. You could only care for one of us.

Ellen. She didn't sit in the chair so much as lean forward from it. Magnuson had seen her last a decade ago, one winter-stunned afternoon when they'd met to sign the settlement.

This time he couldn't keep his hands still. Slowly, as if she were real, he reached out and cupped her cheek.

Last of the Three Ravens
Erin Virgil

People say things like, "He kept one of his wings, that one," and, "Too bad, he was only a child."

My stepmother turned me into a bird. Knit me a shirt from stinging nettles. My arm got stuck going in and stuck coming out. A shirt full of points: when she said certain words, the points turned in, pierced me. Made my skin go from white to blue black. It became a softer texture. Like how a mummy must feel: bound and heavy.

Our sister couldn't speak, this was part of the arrangement.

But why couldn't she write? No paper and no ink in the woods, I suppose. Mouth full of dirt for her; we had a mouth full of feathers, always preening, self-conscious. My brothers don't remember so well. We stayed like ravens for three years, three months, three days. Three minutes early, my sister called out and my black wing is the payment. Three minutes equals one arm on some distant scale.

But the wing's good for pointing. Beckoning, come here.

When I was a raven the feathers grew in and out and I lost them and grew new ones, like hair. Now it's the same five feathers forever.

Seeing the three of us walking together, a man said, "Here come the murder brothers." But we're not crows, we're ravens. The solitary ones, but this time in a little group. Because we were not just ravens, we were ravens that used to be boys.

For buttoning up a coat, I have developed a system. The wing is very useful for brushing snow off windows and fanning new fires. In the hottest part of summer, the feathers stick together, slick with moisture.

The hardest part is trying to hold someone with one arm and one wing. Never feeling balanced. Always at a tilt: do you see how different I am?

Hearing the word anthropomorphic. Glancing down at my pieced together shadow.

"Does the wing still try to fly?" someone asked.

No, but when I see a black bird flying, it twitches.

On the Experience of Rain
Bede Moloney

Many, many years into the future, a citizen of The Red Planet had sent an email to the planet's newspaper editor curious about the lack of information on an almost forgotten weather phenomenon called raining. Little is mentioned of it except in school history textbooks where storms and floods were part of the old Earth's volatile weather patterns. The author wondered what it was like when it rained, and what effect it had on people. Did water really come as rain, he asks, unlike now, when water drips from a huge overhead dome or is packaged as a colorless jelly. It was a really interesting question, setting off a chain of scholarly events leading to the unearthing of old letters in the capital's library that reported actual experiences of rain and its effect on the people.

The letter writers were a people from the West Coast of an unknown island called Tasmania situated south of a larger relatively unknown island, called Australia. The West Coast of Tasmania received a lot of natural rain due to its exposure to the weather patterns of high winds, atmospheric depressions, and changes in sea temperatures, while at the same time the East Coast of Tasmania received very little. Such were the vagaries of the weather and geography that those who needed it most got very little of it, and those who didn't got too much. People from the West Coast who had relatives on the East often wrote them letters describing their experiences of rain. The letters were not written to goad the East Coasters nor make them jealous. On the contrary, they wrote to bolster the spirits of their droughty cousins and also to warn them of the down side of rain; because after the love comes the sorrow.

Some letters told of the bad rains. Putting aside the fact that it often didn't come when it was wanted or it came when unwanted, the intensity of it varied. Sometimes it came as a little sprinkle to be hurried away by the rays of the sun when soon no trace of it remained. At other times the rain wouldn't go away. Not for days, and sometimes not for a whole week. In summer the rain often threatened a human playtime activity called sunbaking, which was a nuisance to the many health conscious West Coasters. Sunbaking was a weekend leisure, where fleshy bodies lay in the baking sun until they reddened and browned, and they then paraded down main streets and into cafes.

And often with rain came high winds, thrusting it at the earth and at people's homes. Then the floods would come and the people wondered if they were being punished for all the wrongs they did. Emergency services were roused; whole communities were forced to get along, and together they saved the homes in which they lived. Afterwards insurance assessors would come and the negotiations for compensation would begin, bringing all combinations of stress and relief to the minds of a damaged people. Rain was like the friend one didn't want to know but couldn't do without.

Other letters told of the greatness of rain, of its wonderfully fresh smell and feel. When it rained greens were greener, soils richer and life august. When a body is wet from rain it electrifies. No air is cleaner than that washed by rain. Rain is like the gentle hand that caresses all fear and anxiety away. Birds bathed and sang in the rain. Playful animals found more ways to play when it rained. And the West Coasters were most inspired when the rains behaved nicely. That is a steady falling rain, periodically in the evening, which turned itself off when it knew the soil and trees, dams and water tanks had got their fill.

The island itself was a hydro (meaning water) economy which obtained its power by mountain and river water being churned through powerful turbines which sat below great dam walls. These dams were mostly situated on the west side of the island. Over time many dams were built to ensure plentiful power for the entire island. And sometimes the government business which provided the power would seed clouds by flying airplanes through them, dispersing silver iodide (a chemical causing ice crystals to form) in order to induce further rain. Not that the West Coasters felt that they needed the extra rain. And yet by being able to induce rain, making it behave nicely, the hydro business said the whole community would benefit. Dams and their offspring the power lines would be central to the prosperity of the island's community. The West Coast inhabitants took the good with the bad. There was some disquiet for a time over the number of dams built, but after a period of unrest Tasmania had become peaceful up until the catastrophe when the forests, those wild suitors of rain, disappeared.

In the interests of the Red Planet's public these old letters were duly published. The planet's citizens know only one climate, the climate of heat. No attempt has been made to control it. The West Coasters of Tasmania wrote about a natural phenomenon they tried to control. It was good for the Red Planet's citizens to know that rain created conflicting feelings of joy and sorrow, despair and hope in their ancestors. They were unlucky. Back then chaos coexisted with order. Too much of nature was out of people's control, which caused great differences. On the Red Planet these emotions are kept repressed due to the brutal consistency of its hot climate. The Red Planet's heat demands its survival. The planet's citizens repress their emotions by making heat irrelevant. And with the letters came the editor's comment that the future of the Red Planet depends on the determined cool adaptation of a very predictable species, and that humans have made great progress since the days of rain.

The Last Velociraptor
Bernard O'Rourke

Professor Rex Green thought that nothing much could surprise him anymore. That was until one of his first year students bit him one afternoon after a long day of lectures. Serves me right for drinking in the student bar, was the only thought he could manage in response.

The techno beats buzzed as a slight, wiry seventeen year old stood over him, blood dripping from his half open mouth. Green had just come in here for a single, solitary pint of Guinness after a draining day, and had deliberately chosen a leather couch in the corner to remain out of the way of any of his own students. It hadn't worked.

"So you are real," said the boy before him, "you can bleed after all."

The head of the Paleontology Department could only return his gaze—speechless as the blood ran from the wound on his exposed forearm and pooled on the dirty floor.

"So little is real these days. Most of the people around here don't bleed at all. Most of them just ignore me. I was starting to think I was the last one left. It isn't good to be left alone like that."

What's Strange

Paul Corman-Roberts

Maybe finding an opossum size cricket bleeding out on my kitchen linoleum wasn't the strangest part. Or maybe it was strange the way it felt like it was reading my mind as I stared at its dying immobilization; a critical nervous function damaged causing its mandibles to slowly flex open and shut as if trying to speak.

Perhaps stranger than that was the way it stared back at me, almost communicating some strange empathy across the short space between us, looking more like an extraterrestrial sentience inhabiting a carapace UFO. Or the vibrato squeal the mutant emitted just before my 21 pound Maine Coon Cat finally finished off the job he started, which I then cleaned up; maybe that was stranger still.

I took the specimen to the taxidermist the next day. One week later she assured me by phone that I could pick up my preserved specimen in two days. Two days later, I arrived at the taxidermist's shop to find the building shuttered and empty, with no forwarding address or contact information. The phone number kept dropping into a voice mail that never picked up.

Now that was fucking strange.

The Detritus

Nancy Stohlman

She feared her husband's death. Though perfectly healthy now, he was sixteen years her senior, and simple math made it apparent he was going to leave her well before she was ready. The idea was so terrifying that she secretly wished to die first. "When I die, will you name a park bench after me?" she would ask him on random occasions, or "If I die first, will you marry again?" And he would look at her gently and say, "Baby, when you die, I'll already be long gone."

She became so obsessed with this preordained tragedy and the dreaded, empty future without him that she began to secretly collect pieces of him—silvery hairs left tangled in the comforter, bits of skin left as dust on the mantle, the crusted toothpaste scraped from the toothbrush, the remnants of wadded up toilet paper from the garbage, stubble wiped from the razor. Each year her collection grew larger.

On the day it happened she was ready; using the

surfeit of collected pieces from her dead husband she immediately constructed him again. In this way she was able to avoid even a single morning of the terror she had feared.

Her new husband was identical to the old; he fit so perfectly into the space left behind that she soon forgot there had ever been a breech. He came with all the idiosyncrasies of the other, all the habits good and bad. They were so identical, in fact, that she began to wonder: Could I alter just a few tiny things? It would be just as easy to make him throw his yogurt containers in the garbage, for instance. Soon her new husband was doing things he'd never done in real life—not falling asleep with all the lights on, spooning with her endlessly all night long, brushing out her hair, reading side by side with her in bed, vacuuming the stairs, ignoring his collection of spaghetti westerns. He was perfect, she thought one morning while he frothed a perfect cappuccino with perfect poached eggs. It was only then that the loneliness she had been avoiding finally found her.

Prompts

1. Using "The Syndicate" as a model, imagine a job that you have no evidence actually exists, and create a character who has this job.

2. As in "The Monstrosity," write a piece where one character has a freakish deformity and another character is attracted to this deformity.

3. "Acts of Faith," is fueled by the metaphor of a "tiny acrobat steadying himself soundlessly on a tightrope strung from my heart to yours while we slept." Write a metaphor that takes over your story.

4. Record your dreams every morning for a week, writing down everything you can remember before you step out of bed. Look for connective threads or reoccurring images and write a story based on one or more of these dreams, looking to "Three Visitors" and "Somnium of Posterus Somnium" as models.

5. Create a story that begins with a fairly common impulse, such as not wanting to be left alone when your husband dies as in "The Detritus" or thinking a child is so adorable that you could just devour them, as in "Inherited Tastes." Take the story to a vividly surreal conclusion.

History and (Pop) Culture

Quick! Where were you when the Challenger blew up, when OJ was found "not guilty," or when you first watched "Thriller"? The way news has been disseminated as a bombardment of images creates a shared experience and nostalgia through media. Andy Warhol, the king of pop culture, said, "Isn't life a series of images that change as they repeat themselves?" Citizens of the 21st Century are particularly caught in the churn of mass media influence and the emulsion of high and low culture. This section, whether exploring the history of what makes us who we are, investigating how we respond collectively to individual artistic expressions, or examining how we define ourselves in terms of objects or trends, fastens our shared experiences to culture.

I'm Pretty Sure Nicolas Cage is my Gynecologist
Kona Morris

I really am. His nose is a little different, but it's probably one of those prosthetic molds they use for the movies, so he can get away with it. He's got the exact head shape, smooth vampire hair, intense eyes, scrunched eyebrow wrinkles, large-lipped open mouth. His height, body, and posture are all spot on—the hunched forward shoulders, long gangly arms. And I would know that voice anywhere, always sounding like there's a yawn trapped behind it waiting to come out. Only, instead of saying, "I came here to drink myself to death," he says, "Alright, just relax back. Oh yes, this is a very healthy looking vagina. Okay, now I'm going to put my fingers on you. Do they feel cold? Okay, now I'm going to insert them." It's very nerve-wracking to have Nicolas Cage's fingers inside me.

Every once in a while during the preliminary exam, he has a burst of spastic energy that causes him to launch across the room and intensely run his hand through his hair. When he's a gynecologist, he behaves a lot more like he did in his old films. There's a sweet crack in his voice, a criminal twinkle in his eyes, and his movements are enchanting as they shift from energetic spasms to sedated and slouching.

I imagine I'm Kathleen Turner in *Peggy Sue Got Married* and he's pacing back and forth in my parents' basement. "Look, I've got the hair. I've got the teeth. I've got the eyes. Peggy, look outside that window. I've got the car. I'm the lead singer. I'm the man." He is convincing and I almost fall for him, but then I realize he is actually flipping through my chart and asking me what kind of birth control I use. I can hardly answer I'm so distracted by his presence. I want to tell him I'm barren, a rocky place where his seed can find no purchase. I want him to do impossibly sweet things for me like climb up ladders and steal babies.

There's a hint of frozen sadness in his expression, something gray in the skin and frightened behind his eyes. I wonder if it's because of all the horrible movies he's done in the last ten years and how obvious it is that they were just for the money. I want to hug him and tell him it's okay—that he redeemed himself in *Bad Lieutenant: Port of Call New Orleans*. That we can forget about *Ghost Rider* now and move on.

When he's got his two fingers pressing against my fallopian tubes, his eyebrows say it all. They shift smoothly, the skin in between them rising and falling. His face tilts slightly to one side and his lower lip drops down, pausing in that second before speech in the way only he can, holding it still for what feels like an eternity.

His eyes are soft and shining as they look at

me over my spread gown covered legs. They make me giggle because of their sincerity. This causes awkwardness for him, like he is suddenly aware that I know who he is, the façade of being a doctor has vanished, and now he is just a famous actor with his fingers deep inside a random woman's vaginal cavity. He diverts his vision, pulls out, and slaps his latex glove off and into the trash in one fell swoop with a quick hop to the other side of the room. He starts to mumble, shuffle, stutter, "I... I... I have to go grab the speculum." His tone is mysterious and breathy, with hints of unnecessary apology, like the self-conscious Charlie Kaufman in *Adaptation*.

When he comes back he has collected himself, but he is rushing. He no longer makes eye contact with me. He seems anxious, like when he woke from the dream about how he had unleashed the lone biker of the apocalypse after Florence Arizona found her little Nathan gone, but he dives back in anyway. He jams the tool far up inside and clicks it shut on the nose end of my cervix. It's pinching and burning as he uses the long, slender swab to collect enough slime to test. I try to say something to show him that I'm okay with who he is, that I don't need a real gynecologist, an actor is fine with me, but then he is gone, taking my pap smear with him.

In it to Win

Robert Vaughan

First Quarter

I really thought his name was Orange Juice. He could run fast, the way he looked in that Buffalo Bills uniform. Oh Jay, "The Juice" made my heart beat faster. I was nearly ten when he appeared in a TV commercial for Hertz rental cars. He smiled, teeth Pepsodent white. His 'fro a perfect halo.

"Such a nice fellow," my mother said.

He was the desired neighbor who never existed in our lily white world.

Second Quarter

"Who are the police chasing?" Susan asked, pointing.

We were waiting for our laundry to dry at Soapy Suds in the Castro. The darks were taking extra quarters to finish. And the lady was trying to find my favorite white wool sweater that I'd dry-cleaned.

The television, mounted in one corner, showed

a dozen L.A.P.D. cars on a low speed chase, sirens blasting. They pursued a white Ford Bronco on the freeway. I glanced outside, a crowd had gathered on that warm June day, watching the TV.

I squinted, trying to read the scrolling letters across the bottom. My jaw flew open. "Holy shit, it's O.J. Simpson."

Susan stopped folding our dark load. "He's a fugitive!" she smirked.

I was clueless, the air drained from the room. "But…why?"

She looked at me point blank. "You didn't hear? He killed his wife."

Third Quarter

The day that he got off, we were all assembled in the boardroom: VPs with secretaries, the artists and education department on one end. Sales, marketing, finance on the other. Some corporate suits lounged in cushy chairs around the massive ebony oblong table. "They're calling this the trial of the century," Netsa whispered.

I nodded. We'd watched the trial televised on court TV all blistering white heat summer. My heart raced. The flat screen TV announced the verdict: Not Guilty.

Netsa grabbed my arm. We drew in a collective groan: shocked, dismayed, bewildered.

All except Lily Roy who shouted, "YAY!" Her fist pumped as high, like it might punch through the ceiling.

Fourth Quarter

Another touchdown scored. He won the game, got away with it. Acquitted.

Or…did he?

"Can you believe it?" my mother scrawled in a card. "He's in trouble…again. But this time around they got him. He's in prison. How are you?"

I knew mom had meant O.J., as I traipsed across my black-and-white tile floor. Was this the sentence he deserved, I wondered. Karma, for an act of malice, or a drug induced spree? Murdering his divorced spouse and best friend. A killer: more Othello than Manson. Still, how do you live with yourself after such Shakespearean drama? Such odious choices.

Pull the wool.

Drink your juice.

Score.

The Final Frontier
Phil Reece

A few weeks ago I read an article in *The New York Times*, "The Spirit of the Space Suit" by Nicholas de Monchaux, about the last space shuttle mission and the significance of the space program.

De Monchaux's point of departure for his reflections was the space suits worn on the moon. For a period of time he was a research fellow at the National Air and Space Museum in Washington D.C. where the suits were stored. I have memories of those same suits. It was 1969 and I was fourteen years old. I grew up in Punchbowl, a western suburb of Sydney. I lived in a fibro house, freezing cold in winter and overheated in summer.

I sat hunched over the smallest of kerosene heaters glued to the TV set, watching fuzzy black and white images. I saw Armstrong step out on to the surface of the moon. He wore a bulky white space suit with a big backpack, an oversized helmet, and on his feet a pair of rippled-soled boots. This was an adventure straight out of a comic book. In the front bedroom of my house another adventure of sorts was unfolding. Hamlet described it as a journey into the undiscovered country. My father lay dying. There was no suit of Teflon and Lycra to insulate him from the cosmic rays of the approaching light. There was no visor to shield his face from the sun hovering on the horizon. There was no oxygen supply to provide him with an atmosphere. All he had was a set of striped pajamas that hung loosely on his skeletal frame. There were buttons missing from his pajama top and it was open and his feet were bare. I remember his yellow skin and sunken cheeks. The disease was eating him from the inside out until there was nothing left. His adventure was not beamed around the world. He travelled alone and in silence.

The two events are now fused in my mind, the spaceman in his generous white suit and my father, little more than a skeleton in his striped pajamas. They are hugging each other as they drift above the moon floating off into the dark and the emptiness.

Touchdown Jesus
Adam Hofbauer

Just north of where I grew up, outside of Cincinnati, Ohio, a church built a statue of Jesus. I have photographs of my father standing by the ten foot tall hand, before they raised it on the frame. He regards it with consternation, the grasping fingers reaching out for him like some kind of theist King Kong. They built it out of Styrofoam and fiber glass, and when it was done it was sixty feet tall. It starts at the waist, so most of that height was arms, raised over Interstate Highway 71 in an, "It's good," kind of gesture that earned him the name Touchdown Jesus. He overlooked the highway for years, keeping score maybe from the end of a reflecting pond filled with fish. Until a few summers ago. When one of those booming mid-western thunder storms came in across it all. Lightning came down, because that's what lightning does, and one of the strikes came in for Touchdown Jesus. All that Styrofoam went up in flames, because that's what Styrofoam does when you strike it with lightning. Poor Touchdown Jesus lit right up, burning there by the side of the highway. In less than a few minutes he was gone, just a charred metal frame casting weird shadows on a fire scarred amphitheater. As a nice little punch line for the Age of Aquarius people, Jesus melted into a big puddle of pious glop. He flowed downhill and into his reflecting pond, and he killed all his fish. And yes, the Church will build another, bigger this time, out of concrete and stone. It would take an earthquake to knock it over. Some might call that security. I call that asking for it.

Virgin Debacle
Meg Tuite

Name: Gladys Piedmont, 22 years old. I had braces and sweaty, brown hair. Gladys was immobilized in time with tiny teeth umbrella-ed under swollen gums, a blonde tragedy of wafting cotton candy over her head, but you had to take what you could get from the one guy in town who sold IDs for ten bucks. I poofed my plastered hair up as best I could.

I hurried to meet Jackie, who was shivering on our designated corner. We'd never studied this hard for any test in our lives. We exchanged fake IDs and quizzed each other. A block away, Jackie pulled out her cosmetic bag and worked over my face. She smudged my face with various colors until she was satisfied. "Now, we're ready."

"If the bouncer asks you anything, act like it's no big thing." We were shaking, but the cold weather masqueraded anxiety as cold-let-me-inside-that-warm-bar-now kind of trembling. I opened the door to "The Ritz." It was the skank bar that let minors in.

I took a quick inventory. One bartender lit up behind the bar poured shots for a few guys. Eyes lingered as I grabbed Jackie's arm and headed for two bar stools.

We had our IDs out. The bartender put up his hand.

"Less I know, the better. What'll it be?"

"I'll have a slow-gin fizz," I said.

"Make that two."

I hoped it didn't taste like that gin sludge my mother drank.

We sucked on drinks, took off our coats to show our three-hour-getting-our-asses-ready outfits. We were drinking in a damn bar.

Some older guys from high school walked over. We lit up cigarettes. Two more drinks were lined up. I was feeling good after some shots and a lot of stupid conversation about school and sports. A few more fizzes with the group and I staggered off to the bathroom.

I didn't wear make-up, so tonight was a whole new face. Jackie had slathered my eyelids with blue, my mouth was sweating some kind of glossy pink. I had black outlines around my eyes. I looked hot. I leaned over and tossed my hair around until I was afraid I'd be in the stall tossing drinks. I was having sex tonight. It was between Jimmy and that dropout, Dave.

I sashayed out trying to look sultry and unwasted. Jackie was giggling with Dave, so Jimmy it was. I smiled without showing my braces. It had been a closed smile for over a year. He grinned one long-toothed-missing-a-few-side-teeth grin. "You wanna sit with me at a back table? Get you another drink?" This was Jimmy's fourth attempt at senior year.

"Yeah," I said. Jimmy brought a tray over with two more shots, a fizz for me and a beer for him. We doused them pretty quick. The small talk was over and there had never been anything large, so we just opened our mouths and got down to business. I hadn't done much tongue action before so I just moved my tongue around like a gyrating snake and Jimmy seemed to take to it. He was jittering his around too, but soon his hand was on my right boob kneading it around in a clockwise direction in time with his tongue like my mother making bread. Jimmy suggested we make a break for his truck. I knew he had a hard-on. He kept putting my hand on it and rubbing it. As soon as he'd let go of my hand I'd let go of his crotch. It was too much juggling and jiggling.

Jackie and Dave were really going at it. I'd lost track of time. Jimmy had my hand on his package again. I pushed him and slurred, "Hold on. I gotta talk to my friend." Jimmy grinned and said, "Hurry up honey, we don't have all night." It was a bad-made-for-TV movie but I was starring, so what the hell.

I started to get up, but noticed a paunchy, red-faced woman stagger up to the bar. She yanked Jackie's long hair. "Listen, you little whore! Get your scrawny ass off this barstool, now!" Jackie's face evaporated all make-up into oblivion. She slunk silently out the door. Jackie's drunken mom was wearing her sleazy nightgown with a coat thrown over it.

"Who the hell do you think you're dealing with?" Jackie's mom screamed. "I'll have this piece of shit establishment closed down so fast, you lowlife hillbillies!" I hid my head in Jimmy's shirt. I watched her stumble around with her index finger pointing in the air. "That girl is sixteen! I'll sue your asses, you mongrels!" She smacked at Dave. "I'll bloody cut your balls off." Dave gave her the finger. "Fuck off, old lady." He started walking toward us.

That's when Jackie's mom spotted me. We looked directly into each other's bloodshot eyes. She started lurching toward me growling, "Well, if it isn't another baby whore getting humped. Get up Tracy and get in the car, NOW!" She lunged at me, but Jimmy caught her.

"Listen, you old bag," Jimmy started. Jackie's mom jumped like a jackal, scratching at his face and eyes. The bartender grabbed Jackie's mom, pulled her off of him. I ran to the door as they were stuffing her into her car. She was smacking at Jackie who was sitting in the back seat as they sped off.

All eyes were on me. "Looks like it's time for you to go," said the bartender. Jimmy didn't even follow me out.

I staggered through the streets knowing my mom was going to get a call from some drunken bag screaming about whores and bars. I took snow and wiped the make-up off of my face. I didn't even feel the cold. When I got to the house the lights were still on. I took a deep breath, pulled off my mittens and put my key in the lock.

Ball, Shark, Pool, and C-3PO   *Jon Olsen*

When I was very young, maybe four years old, my mother and her second husband changed their names and mine illegally so my biological father wouldn't find me, and we all moved to Los Angeles. My only memories of Los Angeles are of the ball and the shark.

The ball was inflatable and streaked with peach and amber hues, and looked, to my eyes, like the planet Venus. Immediately upon jumping out of the car, when we parked in front of our new home in Echo Park, I grabbed the ball and exuberantly threw it at the ground. The ball bounced mightily into the air, and then bounded down the steep street like an escaped gazelle, disappearing from my life forever.

The shark was a foot long, white, and made of Styrofoam. It was hollow, and had a coin slot on its back, just ahead of the dorsal fin. I remember sitting on a linoleum floor and playing with the shark while listening to the Rankin-Bass production of *The Hobbit* on vinyl. I do not recall it being a part of my existence after Los Angeles. The only reason I remember it at all is because a photograph of me playing with it, dug out of a box of old papers hidden in a closet, sparked my memory.

A few months later, we hastily moved to a remote part of northern California, into a trailer near transmitter towers that hummed and swayed in the powerful winds. This is where I remember having the pool and C-3PO.

The pool was an ordinary plastic kiddie pool. In the hot summer months, it was filled with water, and I spent hours dunking toy dinosaurs in it. Then the weather got colder, mosquitoes started spawning, and so my mother dumped the water out. On one exceptionally windy day, the pool was lifted off the ground and carried far away over the hills, like Dorothy Gale's house in the twister.

C-3PO may have been the only toy I still had from my previous life, a gift from my biological father before he faded into legend, becoming a bogeyman in my mother's fairy tales of psychotic domestic violence. All I know is this: I fell asleep in my bed holding C-3PO in my hand. In my dream I was still clutching him tightly in my fingers, but when I woke up he was gone. I dug through the clutter in my room over and over again, but I never found him. Years later, I still have dreams that I'm holding him tight in my hand, only to feel him dissolve into nothingness as I wake up.

Prompts

1. Using "The Final Frontier" and "In it to Win" as models, juxtapose images of history or pop culture with more personal events.

2. Read "Virgin Debacle." Many of us had fake IDs and underage drinking experiences. Write a story based on a fake ID.

3. Write the name of a specific location. Next, write the name of a celebrity, the first that pops into your mind. Now write from the point of view of a first-person narrator interacting with the celebrity without leaving that location, as occurs in "I'm Pretty Sure Nicolas Cage is My Gynecologist."

4. Find a statue in your hometown and write a story around that statue, using "Touchdown Jesus" for inspiration.

Prompts

5. Remember a specific childhood toy that was lost, as occurs in "Ball, Shark, Pool, and C-3PO." Write a story that contemplates its disappearance.

Hybrids and Hermaphrodites

One of the pleasures of flash fiction is how it blurs the boundaries of genre, using the sensitivity to language usually displayed by poets where each word needs to be precisely the right one, and sometimes the sounds of words together is more important than what they add up to. Where a prose poem stops being a prose poem and starts being a flash fiction piece has been a matter of much literary debate with no conclusive answers but many interesting questions. This section showcases experiments in form; the prompts included are intended to help move writers away from their conception of themselves as writers within a particular genre and toward experimentation and cross-genre hybridization.

Distillation
Sacha Siskonen

I.

We ditched school to go to the museum. We ditched grad school to go to the art museum. We ditched an optional, extracurricular lecture to go to the modern wing of the Art Institute of Chicago. A friend and I wandered the bright, white galleries tilting our heads back and forth in a thoughtful posture as we contemplated the paintings hung on the walls. She and I stopped in front of the Dalis, and did not cup our chins, or put our index fingers to our temples, but easily could have. I was never taken to art museums as a child. Though, my father sometimes took us to the Museum of Natural History in Manhattan so my sister could see the dinosaur bones. The first Dali I ever saw was a poster on a dorm room wall.

Two women crossed in front of us in the gallery. One, younger, pushed the other in a wheelchair. I watched them pass by—a moving sculpture. The woman in the wheelchair asked to stop, wanted to linger in front of *Inventions of the Monsters* for a moment. The other refused. She kept walking, past the painting, pushed the woman out of the gallery without pause. My friend and I exchanged a glance. How cruel. How monstrous. How could anyone do such a thing? A brute. A bully. The mean little moment stuck with me. Caught in my teeth.

II.

A woman pushed her elderly mother through the galleries in a wheelchair. They moved swiftly, floating across the floor. The wheelchair belonged to the museum. The mother had not wanted to borrow it, saying, "I'll just shuffle along." But the woman had insisted. Was this a kindness or an exertion of power? Can we ever be sure? The picture windows let in the light. Outside the city stood shining. Glass, concrete, brick, steel, sky, marble, sun. The gilt top of a skyscraper glinted in the afternoon light. The woman, sturdy and sweat-shirted held her lips tight together, a thin line, pinked and pursed. In the wheelchair, the mother looked wide-eyed at the paintings. She considered her perspective. Lower now from the chair, altered in this one small way, but what a difference it made. She couldn't see the tops of things. Couldn't take her own steps.

Across the room she saw the Dalis on the wall. Clocks melted, pianos deflated, a tiny giraffe stumbled, its neck on fire—a flaming mane. The distorted bodies, the figures cut in half, breasts bared. It made her think of giving birth. The open space, the arid landscape, the pain. She had been connected to some vast and eternal life force, given the divine power of creation for a day, well, thirty-four hours. But Dali couldn't have known it. He wasn't trying to paint what she saw. It was an accident. Something only she could see from her seat in the wheelchair. She thought she might not have seen it at all if she had been able to stand. Everything would seem different.

Her daughter pushed her past whispering tourists with cameras in front of their faces, sleepy-looking guards, a troop of uniformed school children who momentarily blocked her view of the painting across the room. Her daughter frowned perpetually. She looked away from the nudes. *Vulgar*, she thought. She couldn't stand to see any depiction of pain. *Gratuitous*, she scoffed. The mother looked and looked.

"Stop and look at this," the mother said. She pointed from her wheelchair at *Inventions of the Monsters* there on the wall before them.

Her daughter kept pushing, past the painting, out of the room. "I am not going to stop and look at it."

III.
On Seeing *Inventions of the Monsters*, 1937

The question becomes is the giraffe on fire, or ablaze, engulfed in flames, or fueled by them?

If the former, there's destruction, an apocalyptic plane. Consumed, wrought, wrecked, he wanes.

If the latter, he retains some level of agency—
he waxes phoenix-like, flaming mane aflame.

How we understand the fire, how we read the differences between *ignite* and *combust*, tells

us how we see the world, both his and our own; yet, I cannot help but think, this looks like home.

The Rod of Correction
Nate Jordon

Spare the rod, spoil the child.

I'll be damned if that wasn't the one and only justification my God-fearing mother needed to beat the hell out of me for eating a spoonful of peanut butter without asking or forgetting to pick up a sock behind my toy box.

Throughout my childhood I'd get backhands to the face for reasons so trivial I laugh when I think about it. And thank Buddha I can laugh about it. I'm in my mid-thirties and flinch so hard at the slightest hand motion in my direction it's difficult to get a haircut or even shave.

According to the King James Version of the Holy Bible, below are the reasons why you should beat the hell out of your kid:

Proverbs 13:24

He that spareth his rod hateth his son: but he that loveth him chasteneth him betimes.

Proverbs 22:15

Foolishness is bound up in the heart of a child,

but the rod of correction shall drive it far *from him*.

Proverbs 23:13

Withhold not correction from the child: for if thou beatest him with the rod, he shall not die.

Proverbs 23:14

Thou shalt beat him with the rod, and shalt deliver his soul from hell.

Proverbs 29:15

Thy rod and reproof give wisdom, but a child left to himself bringeth his mother to shame.

None of this should come as a surprise. For Christ's sake, God let his only begotten son get beaten to a blood dripping pulp and get crucified . . . all for conducting a few miracles and loving his neighbor. Maybe I got it easy. Maybe I should have been drawn and quartered for the mortal sin of eating a cookie without asking first.

By the time I was in second grade, my mother had been slapping me around so much she got tired. She had to convince my stepdad to do the beating. She used the Good Book on him too, telling him he's the man of the house and therefore had to be the disciplinarian and in the meantime he'd better get off the La-Z-Boy and stop slurping Raisin Bran on Sunday mornings and go to church. But he didn't have the heart to beat me. He wasn't evil and he wasn't insane which is why he didn't need to go get preached at in order to salve his own inner bullshit. He was just a guy who sold cars, watched golf on TV, and smoked too many Kent III's.

To keep from beating me, and keep my mother at bay, he saw a doctor who wrote him a note saying his palms were sensitive and frequent spankings would break the blood vessels in his hands. This he gave to my mother who, after reading it, smirked, sniffed through one dilated nostril, and quipped, "There's always the belt."

The belt didn't last long and neither did my stepdad. My mother had to find a husband who had no problems with righteous violence. She found this psycho at a church.

Cordell was a 6' 6" balding German weighing over 240 pounds, worked construction, was a deacon at Christian Life Ministries, and had a moustache that made Tom Selleck's confess its sins. Shortly after moving into Cordell's rickety Houston home, I walked into the garage from the kitchen and saw Cordell kick his boot into my dog's chops.

I'd been wondering why Ralph, a big male Doberman, was always quaking in fear. And there it was. Enough boots to the face will turn anything into a quivering milksop.

I told my mother about this but she didn't see the problem. Cordell was a man of God and therefore was in his right to do whatever he, or their so-called God, felt was correct. In Cordell my mother not only found a man who enjoyed kicking dogs, but also enjoyed beating me, and . . . oops . . . had no problem beating her either. Which he did, frequently, for many years, until that rainy night when he tackled my mother in the street and just after slamming her face into the asphalt, heard my .410 shotgun cock.

They found this to be good reason for divorce.

The beatings stopped but I soon missed them. They taught me things. They taught me something about Jesus. Jesus got beat to shit and learned mankind is stupid and weak.

After thousands of years, you'd think we could do better.

A Trip to the Store
Roberta Hartling Gates

Part 1: My Husband's Brother

"Come with me to the store," he had said, so I went. Not that I needed anything, but Brad was like that, just a big overgrown kid: privacy meant nothing to him. He was my husband's brother, a young guy just out of the service. Everywhere he went, he was so thrilled just to be wearing regular clothes, no uniforms or saluting or anything else, that he bounced when he walked.

In Aisle 7 of the store, he picked up a bottle of shampoo. "Is this any good?" he asked. "Does it really add body? Show me what you like."

Whenever I turned around, he was throwing something else into the cart: steaks two inches thick, sour cream for baked potatoes, one each of all the Ben and Jerry's flavors that were new to him. It worried me to see all that stuff piling up, but Brad was casual about it: "Hey, I've got money," he said.

At the check-out counter, he had to have Tic-Tacs

and one of those little crossword puzzle books that they keep in the racks. He said he was giving them to me and I laughed. He was just so crazy.

The cashier was so young she had to holler "twenty-one" to get our beer rung up.

She kept looking at Brad and asking him things: Did he want paper or plastic? Did he know that this or that item was a buy-two-get-one-free? Of course he had no idea. He just kept shrugging his shoulders and smiling that smile of his, his teeth as perfect and white as Chiclets.

Heading home, he drove slowly, with all the windows down. The day was warm, almost like summer, and the air had a fresh, moist smell. Brad was punching buttons on the radio, and I was just riding along, my eyes half-closed.

Then I felt his hand on my knee. I opened my eyes and stared at it as if it had fallen from space. The little reddish-blond hairs that grew across the back of it gleamed like copper in the sun. "Ben can be a real bastard," he was saying. "I lived with him, so I should know."

"No, you don't," I said, the hot wind blowing into my face, slapping around my hair. "You don't know anything."

"Lisa, you don't have to lie to me," he said then. "I know. I know what he does to you."

I looked at him, but the words banging together in my head were too loud; I had to turn away. All around us, the cars streamed by, either dark blue or black, their colors so shiny they looked wet. I'd been crying all along, I guess, but until I picked up his hand and kissed it, the tears had been inside. Yes, I thought, watching them fall over his coppery hand: Yes, finally, someone had seen.

Part 2: My Brother's Wife

Ben had always gone for dark roots and gloppy eye makeup—a certain kind of grittiness that he could get hold of and squeeze. Lisa wasn't like that, though: she was ordinary, an ordinary girl with small high breasts and hair that fell over her face. But for a newlywed she seemed sad. You could see it in her eyes, how watchful they were, wary almost.

Then one day Ben was out somewhere. "Come with me to the store," I said. I'd been at their house for almost a week by that time, and I wanted to get her out of there.

We went to a supermarket so big you could have parked airplanes in it, but she was like a pro, she knew her way around. Walking up and down the aisles with her, watching that sweet little butt of hers as she pushed the cart along, I wondered if people thought maybe we were the ones who were married. I wanted to buy her things: some steaks, expensive shampoo, Tic-Tacs, whatever. She was humoring me, probably because she thought I was still a kid. It irritated me, but I forgave her. It was good just to hear her laugh. On the way back, with warm, bright air coming in through the car windows, it killed me to have her sitting right there next to me, wearing those cute little jean shorts of hers. I leaned forward and messed with the radio. I was close enough to smell her hair, which was sunny and citrusy. I longed to do or say something that was real. Finally, a Beatles tune came up and I let my hand drop to her knee. If she'd been startled, I would have pulled it away fast, but she was calm.

"Ben can be a real bastard," I said, afraid to look at her. Beneath my hand, her kneecap felt fragile and small. "I lived with him," I added, "so I should know."

"No, you don't," she said. "You don't know anything." But her voice was sort of broken, and I guessed she was trying not to cry.

"Lisa, you don't have to lie to me," I said. "I know what he does to you."

Beside me, on the seat, she was still, quiet, like an animal that's folded itself away. What kind of dope was I? I wondered, as a semi rushed by, its slipstream sucking at us. Why had I said that? And if I was going to say it, why hadn't I built up to it more?

But then, just as I was about to lift my hand away, she snatched it up and pressed it to her lips. She was crying, but there was no sound. The tears fell onto the back of my hand, washing it. They scared me a little, those tears, but I was young then, I thought I could fix anything.

He Broke Pictures
Carolyn Zaikowski

Still he broke pictures of me with the best of them. With the dark of his hand in the river, he worked hard, and in a lonely fashion. He was farther now, downstream, in a crevice somewhere near a purpose and a vein, neither of which I would ever know. It had really happened, this unspeakable opposite. His whisper had gotten fainter until it could not be distinguished from a leaf batting at a window like a paw, or a pine cone falling against a stump's moss. And all along I'd believed that it was the water's job to speak. That there had to be room for something other than this wading, washing, and falling ashore. But really it was just there to tell you what you were reflecting. To get you to ask the fine questions of yourself. And now I spoke and expected a reply, and expected an answer, and expected him as he'd entered all those times. But I found only myself there, dripping. I tried to take you home but you fought back, I said, quietly now, perhaps with a fingertip of tears. I said, I tried to take you home again but still you fought; and then I tried to fight back, too, but still I could not take you home. No matter how many pages of mine you tossed over your brink, and no matter how I tried, no matter how gracefully I danced along your edges to the shore that was actually mine, I could not hold you for as long as it would have taken to take you home.

45-Year Rain
Kathryn Winograd

I think of the women who leave / the sky throwing down its great shining cabbage leafs of rain / the whole gray tarp of the world folding down / and those wishing stars spinning like precarious plates calling *here here* / the streets of these women bruising like wet ash / and the stink of oil of shale and lost dinosaur / and those small flattened wings of birds they keep finding and the white hands of the rain/and the lilacs / how they always come / the lilacs / unbearably wet now / our old Jewish neighbors long dead now / reaching their tattooed arms through the hedge groves / and the beautiful German farm woman of my childhood / old now / half-crazed now / in the crazed rain feeding her wounded chickens / my father sitting at the kitchen table / smiling / alive / the whole world of my father alive / not just this beached whale of winter grass / this dried cunt of fifty years / these bones of my mother and her mother's mother dry as tinder / one mis-step and the angel crack of our hips bringing us down / *Angel Face* / *Beauty* / to be kissed once more / I mean really kissed / not just that half-peck shit but the whole flowering /trembling the green haze / the mitosis of cells dividing and dividing the rain / like silver sheets / the rain shining over the hayfields / my windshield wipers like a clock ticking down Coal Mine Avenue / the last dust flying up into the boughs of rain and me / thinking about everything I haven't done or done right /that screwed up garden how easy it seems / to give it all up the rain / the lilacs those dormant suburban bulbs / and even those three coyotes I really did see howling beneath the morning moon in the snow-bent fields and you / whistling softly in the kitchen / staring into the rain above the dishes' steam the rain through the white flower of your face the rain / falling / and the air *I had to leave you* gone / sweet where the rain speaks / and so I don't

Tent

JP Vallières

Things move quickly.

You dream of going places and you go there.

< >

Six years out west.

Your home is a tent if it rains. But mostly a sleeping bag in the dirt. You travel by foot. You take to the great trails, alone.

You forget about college for awhile.

This is when the pale wash of panic around you mysteriously disappears.

You find a French woman doing the same thing as you somewhere deep in the Cascades. When the weather is especially fierce you both go into your tent and hold each other and imagine the tent is a ship in outer space.

She leaves you and immediately you cleave to this great insult. You pack it away in your backpacker's pack. You sleep with it. You carry it up the mountains and along the rivers.

You know this weight will never be completely lifted from you.

You come to a conclusion. You have to. That she is from the future and that this is what French women do.

This is what American women will be doing twenty years from now.

< >

You travel much more on foot. With a big pack.

Nothing can stop you because of how you formed your body. Perfect now for walking many miles carrying lots of pounds.

You don't need that much to eat but when someone offers you food you gorge yourself and feel a surge run through you.

Your body absorbing good earth.

< >

Walking comes to a screeching halt the day you meet a woman in Europe.

Two Americans in Europe, in a café. The only two people in the place who can speak nothing but English.

You laugh at each other's jokes because they sound so funny. They sound funny without accents.

Even if something isn't funny both of you laugh.

You dream together about the future.

And you plan it.

And you go through with it.

< >

Your third child is twelve. When you come home from work you see her and know how fast all of this is.

The other two call and ask for money.

But they also ask about you and mom and their sister. They thank you all the time, actually.

One of them is planning to walk the same trails as you once walked.

You try to find a way to tell him it's not worth it.

< >

You're not dying yet but whenever you see yourself in the mirror you are surprised at what is there, staring back.

Prompts

1. Using "Distillation" as a model, write a piece in three different forms: a micro-essay observing a scene, a short story, and a poem.

2. Weave a mythological text throughout. Use "The Rod of Correction" as an example for interplay between plot and outside sources.

3. Tell a story where there is a clear and distinct split in points of view. Read "A Trip to the Store" for an effective example.

4. Use your own poem or someone else's and convert it into a story, experimenting with line breaks, as in "45-Year Rain." Or convert a story into a poem, using actual line breaks on the page.

5. Tell a story through the form of a list, using a second-person point of view, as in "Tent."

Science, Nature and Place

Notice that one of the common characteristics of flash fiction is that it often depends on a single location to allow for brevity in storytelling, so it is crucial that the setting and environment are well crafted. When a story successfully integrates plot with place, science, ecology, and non-human elements with a riveting story line, the writer has carried out an impressive feat. The stories in this section all successfully marry a strong sense of environment with other masterful elements of storytelling.

Cold Feet
Bryan Jansing

Along the edge of the ice, where the water is not still and will not freeze despite the winter, stands a goose and her mate. All around them are small, familiar mounds.

The night snow has settled upon these mounds like white hospital sheets. Each morning there are new mounds along the edge of the ice where the frigid water laps at them. The mounds are the dead bodies of the Canadian geese who have come to rest overnight, but who will not be leaving in the morning. As winter grips the pond and the occasional goose, the ice becomes a fowl burial ground.

Each morning my wife steps onto our balcony and points out another still goose, "I can't tell if that one is alive."

It is, but the goose has not moved from her place all morning. It seems her feet froze to the icy sub zero night and while the rest of the flock rose with the sun in the morning, she could not follow.

She is alive, but the two geese stand forlorn in the cold day. And though the sun's rays, like warm fingers, melt the snow and ice they touch, the wind bitterly whips at her.

She stands, but does not walk. Her mate encircles her and in their silence they seem to cry her finality. There are no other living geese on the pond. In contrast, the ducks move frantically about, dipping their heads into the chilling water, shaking off the pellets as they form onto their feathers. In a flightless flock, the ducks rush about the ice, waddling desperately for warmth. The gander moves with the ducks to the shore from time to time and he stops to look back as if still encouraging her to keep trying.

We all stand solemnly together as if attending the funeral of a loved one. I think back to the morning and picture her flock rising into the air while she frantically flaps her wings, but does not rise. I recall a dream I had once as a child where my family could fly and flew away and I remained stuck to the earth crying out, "wait, I cannot fly like you".

I shudder and shake the thought from my mind.

Throughout the day, I watch the afternoon push the sun to the west and pull a cold shadow over the goose. All her energy has gone into the ice that now bonds her to the pond. Eventually, she rests her head upon the ice and seems to sleep. She is still alive, but there her body will lie until spring melts winter and ice turns to water. Only then will she sink into the belly of muck that lies beneath her and only then will time devour her. My heart goes out to her mate whom I watch return to her over and over from the shore. The ducks waddle along the ice; web prints stamp the fresh snow all around the imprisoned goose like the steps of mourners at her wake. Her mate is by her side, despite the icy consequences to him and they are still very quiet, unlike geese. Though habit has tuned their noisy flight out of my sleep, their silence makes me strangely weary. They make no squawks to one another, as they must have done on so many migrations, speaking to one another as they flew over countless lakes and foreign lands. Now they are silent and I'm saddened that he cannot tell her comforting words. Perhaps they need none; perhaps their loyalty to one another through the years is enough.

I'm looking at my wife's sad face, rosy with winter's kisses. I think of her feet, her little feet so vulnerable to diabetes, the feet I tenderly massage from time to time to stimulate the warm blood's circulation. They too may one day become stuck in an icy debilitation. I try to summon the words that I might say should the sun's afternoon shadow slide upon her as I stand by her side; strangely, I fall silent too.

Welcome Wharf

Jennifer Springsteen

The boat cuts crystal water, and Margret drops her hand over the side, spreads her fingers, cups her fingers, spreads her fingers. The water pulls, her fingers resist. She sees all the way to the bottom: gold and orange poking anemones, some with poison spikes and weeks of fever. There isn't a seat for her on this fishing trip so she hunches on the floor and tucks her flip flops under Bentley's wooden bench. Every time Bentley or Mr. Triele pull up a net or crab pot, they spill bits of the ocean on the boat's floor. Margret feels like she's peed in her pants. If she could jump in and be all wet, she'd be even. But she's been instructed to sit still. The crabs and lobsters are watchful.

"Get your hand up, girl," says Bentley.

She pulls it up and sucks at her salt fingers. Wrinkles her nose at Bentley. The boat is still. They look out across the tipsy sea and wait.

Mr. Triele whistles a little. His lips are salted over

and he stops mid-tune to lick, then starts in again lazy and low.

Margret doesn't want to be a fisherman, but she wants to be on the boat. She's in love with Mr. Triele, and she wants to be near him.

Mr. Triele has a thin tight neck and long arms like good rope. His palms are wide and deep black with pink wormy scars where a line has caught him or where he was pinched by a fighting crustacean fearing the finality of boiling pots and breaking hands. Usually Mr. Triele can wrap his hands around a crab and hold it firm, without a pinch. He calms them, too.

Margret won't eat the lobsters or crabs. She doesn't like the taste of something pulled angrily from its slumber, claws beating back death. Instead she wants to pull the ocean from Mr. Triele's fingernails. Crack open his hard teeth and lick the cool salty saliva under his tongue. Burrow into his chest and feed there.

Margret stays at Welcome Wharf with her mother. They flew to Jamaica six months ago to escape the embarrassment of her father's indiscreet love affairs. "Who needs ninth grade?" Margret's mother had said with a flick of her wrist, pausing between suitcase and closet. Margret sat on the bed thinking of softball and Jenny Mitchell whispering *lard ass* and teachers ignoring her raised hand. Would anyone remember her?

Mr. Triele and his son Bentley bring fresh fish to the house every other day, and the cooks blow around the kitchen preparing meals for Margret's mother and the tide of sympathetic visitors come to lend support.

Every other day Margret wakes early, brushes her teeth and combs her hair and runs through the palm trees to where their boat sits in the sand. They greet her with a nod, let her climb in the middle before they push the boat into the water.

Bentley has closed his eyes, letting the breeze tickle his lashes. Mr. Triele watches the boy, then puts his calloused palm on Margret's knee. The heat under his hand coils down her thigh, pulls at the hem of her wet shorts, rubs inside her underpants. The crab traps are full and restless—the crabs have found the bait. Bentley flings open his eyes in time to see his father's hand rise from her bony knee, to see Margret returning the smile she had been given. Who would Bentley tell? He and his father move to the nets and pull hand over hand. Splashing water, tilting the boat.

Margret feels the rising in her chest. They are trapped now, all of them caught.

Guide to Dissecting the First Bird of Spring
John Sibley Williams

It will come, regardless. From your window a few scattered buds that seem an insurmountable distance from where you left them will thrust up from their leafless trees, and from beneath a soggy blanket of pine needles the earth will warm. And because this change began with the air, the air will carry along with its southern winds and tirades of hope and green a single bird, often a jay, to beat itself senselessly against the gray sky. The horizon bruises then bleeds then squirts something of cherry juice into your mouth. The bird is imaginary, is suddenly a silhouette, matures into flesh as it lands on the fencepost that separates properties, and you move to meet it halfway between flesh and what it symbolizes, a bundle of knives under your arm. This is a good start. You are outside.

First you must catch the bird, the simplest task, as it will be awaiting your hands. Cup one hand over its beak and collect its voice. Don't let a note slip through your fingers. Ball your hand immediately into a fist, bring your fist to your own open mouth, and swallow. Try calling for your parents, who are still inside, as always. Try calling for your wife and children. Try weeping. Try singing. There is still time to master your voice.

Next, slip a serrated blade into the rich hues of the bird's chest, careful to keep the throat wide. Crack the ribcage and feel around for the heart. There is always a heart; keep feeling. Remove the heart and deposit it in your chest. Inhale. Spring is all around you. Take in its blood.

Next, the wings. Custom dictates a filet knife, though any curved blade will work. Carve off the wings, as you would run your fingers across the hollow of your lover's back at midnight, while she sleeps and dream speaks, just before she turns away. Affix them to your back with string or glue. Contemplate flying. Think about the renewed warmth of your home as it gathers distance.

Cradle this bird you've placed so much faith in and sever its beak. Try it on. Your skin will be ready for the transition. It has been ready for months. This has been your sole dream since that first leaf toppled so many lifetimes ago. Approach your first tree. Speak to it in your shared language. Feel the limbs below you stretch in supplication. Rap your beak into its holes and try to pull sustenance from the dead bark. See if the mites and ants emerge for your new mouth. See if you can find something in nothing.

Finally, decide, arbitrarily yet firmly, that you are now a new man, that nothing will be the same. Winter has not been wasted. Life is upon you again. Your tiny bird heart will reopen in petals. You now have a voice that can greet the light.

Pathetic Fallacy
Susan Lewis

At the support group for violated stones, the quarry brimmed with (silent) strife over the tendency of some to ascribe mineral virtues to animals—including and especially certain bipedal perpetrators of mayhem and havoc. *We have a term for that mistake,* scolded one ancient boulder, sporting more than one dynamite scar. *We know: "the serene impossibility,"* admitted a bright young chunk, veins of quartz sparkling in the dying light. Still, some held out for optimism. *We have seen things,* they insisted. *Humans sitting quietly, gazing into the distance. Another predatory ruse,* scoffed the Elder. *They were probably plotting their next explosion. Unless you think there's nothing to distinguish us from the frenetic vulgarity of the animate. I don't know,* the young one demurred, light winking from its crystalline ridge. *But what if there's another way to look at things?* 'and why should overlap belie uniqueness,' it wanted to ask. But it was intimidated by the Elder's stolid, featureless resolve.

Isn't That True?

Sonja Larsen

In the pet store she's standing in front of the glass aquarium of mice. He's watching the neon tetras, darting back and forth, a long blue and silver stream moving across the tank. He's concentrating on the silver shift, the moment the fish turn and are caught in the light. She stands in his peripheral vision on the other side of the store. From a distance she looks forlorn and dark, her fingers pressed to the glass, like a small child waiting to be noticed.

"Did I ever tell you" she says, "about the baby mice?" He's standing beside her now, the fish food he came in for in his hand. She's watching the mice, pink-fleshed noses crushed against the glass where her fingers touch. Nuzzling, pushing. He can hear their soft squeals.

"The wild mice you caught?"

"One summer, I must have been seven or eight, I decided I wanted mice as pets. We lived in the country then. I set jars baited with food in the wood pile, to catch them."

"You told me."

"They died. All summer. Five or six mice, I caught. And they all died."

He can see the smudges her fingers have made on the glass.

"You told me."

"I'd look in the little cage I built, and they'd be dead. All little and brown. You know, nobody told me to stop. They just let me. Nobody told me they'd keep dying."

She's standing there, near tears over the wild mice. And if it were anything so simple as mice, a sad thing from a long time ago, he would touch her shoulder perhaps, reach out to touch her. But it's something else, not from then, but from now. Not mice, but some other small thing moving in the walls.

"We talked about this," he said.

"Before. And you talked."

"You didn't say anything. You didn't disagree. You knew how I felt about this and you didn't say a thing."

"No," she says, tracing the outline of the mouse's body through the glass, "I didn't."

"What's different now?"

"It," she says. "It's different."

"It is the size of a kidney bean."

"A kidney bean with fingers."

"Oh for Christ sakes," he says too loudly, and the tall thin clerk at the cash register looks over at them, startled.

"Your fish are the size of kidney beans and you care about them," she says. "You don't say there's too many fish in the world but there's way more fish than people." She follows him to the cash register. "Isn't that true?" she asks the cashier. "Isn't it?"

Grid-Lock

Lucy Black

She is wearing a dollar store tiara and we can just see the top of a pink sequined dress—likely a ballet dress or a princess costume. Her black bangs are combed across her forehead and her dark eyes shine brightly as she bounces a little in her seat. We are caught in what appears to be grid-lock and the secondary fan has just kicked in. Trying to keep our car from over heating, we have turned off the air conditioning and opened the windows.

The open windows have somehow made us more vulnerable, more aware of the congestion of the city. Cyclists are stopped alongside the cars, discretely balancing themselves with one hand on the rear flank of the vehicle. Pedestrians are congregated at the corners, waiting to cross at the intersection, and straining to see what the difficulty is; where the accident is; what the hold-up is. I place my purse on the floor between my feet, concerned that someone could easily reach in and pluck it from my lap.

There are two policemen in the middle of the intersection directing traffic. They arrived on bicycles, wearing shorts. The stop lights are working but they are ignoring these and yelling directions at drivers and pedestrians alike. They seem stressed and angry. They speak into walkie-talkies. Collectively, we listen intently, trying to determine where they would like us to move and why.

The car in front of our queue attempts an illegal right turn and is screamed at by the young officer. Slowly the driver reverses his car, and awkwardly repositions himself at the front of our line. We have not yet crept forward to claim the additional six feet of pavement. We wait impatiently and frustrated, trying to understand why we are locked here.

And then it slowly becomes clear. Two police motorcycles approach, followed by a police car with flashing lights. "A politician," states my partner with contempt. "We've all been sitting here in the heat waiting for the f-ing premier to drive by."

My eyes cast over the sidewalk crowd and I see that some of them have also sensed this. They are waving at the motorcade of black cars that are now driving towards us. A parade of large black limos. But then I see the two policemen saluting. Rigid. Standing at attention. A hearse appears and the crowd quiets.

"Of course," I think suddenly, "a fallen soldier."

"What an insult," sputters my mate. "Why the f do they call the trip to the morgue, the *Highway of Heroes*? It's an insult. Why not pick a beautiful road or a national highway? The trip to the morgue? It's ludicrous. What a lack of imagination."

"It's moving," I respond. "The families find it moving. And helpful."

"I'm not denigrating that aspect," he fumed, "it's

just the whole *Highway of Heroes* thing. Why couldn't they pick something less ironic?"

"It's a way to mark gratitude," I respond gently, "it's the least we can do for their families."

"It's not a war we should be fighting. We don't belong there and those boys don't belong there. Canadians should not be dying there."

"But we are there," I say, "and the nation needs to mourn."

"Not like this," he answered, shifting the car into drive, and accelerating slightly. "Not like this."

I look over at the adjacent car, and get a final glimpse of the little girl. She surveys the roadway happily as her car also moves forward. She is still bouncing a little. Untouched by the young man who has died before his time and the pain of those left behind. I press the button to close my window while my partner turns on the air.

Centerville
Donna Laemmlen

Every visit to this town begins in the same way, by driving past a chunk of redwood, the words "Welcome to Centerville, Gateway to the Sequoias" carved into its lacquered bark, revealing the town to be a portal to another place as much as its own destination, making it difficult for the town to craft an identity of its own, its identity as shifting as the string of businesses that have flared through it, leaving behind barren buildings and empty streets, chasing the expanding highways and multiplying subdivisions, imagining it will be better the next time, in that place, on that road.

So when this town cobbled together what was left and went back to the chore of defining who it was, it struggled, stifled by the mishmash of architecture and purpose rising up from Main Street, the terra cotta columns of a former bank now flanking second-hand appliances, the neon drive-in sign buzzing above treadmills and stationary bikes, the marquee of the movie theater advertising used cars. If it hadn't been for the citizens and their persistence in maintaining some semblance of their former life by lining up every morning to buy pastries at the old newspaper office, where they'd exchange ideas for shaping the town's identity, perhaps a farmer's market to replace the desolate packing houses, or a fiesta to bring back the city's diverse culinary talents, the town wouldn't have had any identity at all. The longer they brainstormed, the more the ideas mushroomed, until they imagined a town that could sustain itself simply on the guts and imagination of the few citizens left, a vision just believable enough they began the hard work of turning the deserted bowling alley into a flea market, the empty car lot into a carnival, the defunct library into a haunted house.

Soon, the town settled into a meager yet comfortable rhythm, slowly regaining a sense of purpose and well-being, the citizens confident they had managed their crisis as well as the town council would have, if they still had one. It wasn't until they gathered along Main Street for the Fourth of July parade that their optimism faltered again. In spite of having allowed fireworks inside the city limits and the selling of beer on the sidewalks, their celebratory spirit plummeted when they saw the parade itself, a parade gutted of its purpose, to showcase the high school band marching at the front, trumpeting the floats covered in metallic fringe and glittery Styrofoam cut-outs, representing the Boy and Girl Scouts of America, the Parent-Teacher Association, the 4-H club and the Order of Odd Fellows, the Chamber of Commerce in their restored Chevys, the policemen touting their sirens and the firemen their shiny red trucks. They were all gone, relocated, disbanded, dissolved.

So empty was the parade the citizens were left with only each other to watch, and since they still had their beers, they did so intently, intently remembering until they began to see themselves in each other and moved across the street to shake hands, not too unlike any other day of the week, only now they shook hands with their younger selves, on their way to deposit money at the used-furniture store or to mail a package at the corner bar, carrying their bowling balls to the flea market or their overdue books to the haunted house, all moving with such purpose they finally understood: the portal hadn't been to the Sequoias after all. It had been to the town itself.

In joyous recognition of this hard-earned lesson, they made dates with each other to celebrate their new independence, some to eat caramel sundaes at the gym, others to watch a double-feature in the used car sales room, and still others to buy champagne at the wedding dress shop, having all agreed to meet back on Main Street by midnight, where the parade would resume, but this time, the citizens themselves would march, banded together as their own float, carrying giant sparklers and covered in crepe paper streamers of red, white and blue.

Feeding the Birds

Kirby Wright

I'm standing at the screen door of my parent's old bedroom: my mother's out back with the birds. There's the usual riot of chirps. "Plenty for all," she promises, under-handing like a softball pitcher. Mom looks silly tossing in a pink muumuu and heels. She throws pieces of stale hotdog buns, scattering widely over the lawn. Even doves have a chance. "You've had enough," she tells an aggressive myna. The doves are her favorites. Once she got a crush on a mallard and bought him his own bag of birdseed. She believes a blood-red cardinal with a bum leg is the reincarnation of Daddy. "Here's some for you," she coos to a skinny sparrow.

A plastic litter box filled with water is perched on a stone. When the cat died the birds got a birdbath. Toads love it. The birds won't bathe or even drink if the toads are swimming. "You get out," Mom scolds.

"Did you see you-know-who?" I ask when she comes inside.

"No," she answers, lowering her eyes. Her hair is as white as an egret.

"Maybe he's on vacation."

She nods and offers a half-smile. "Daddy sure liked to travel."

I see hopping outside—a black toad bounces over the grass like a crazed shadow. I think he's heading for the ferns. A family of apricot finches takes flight.

Burning Out

Matthew Purdy

The papers said a star would die tonight. We heard some people were having parties to watch it disappear, so we invited Greg and Nancy over for a barbecue. Besides, it was the weekend; it was a thing to do. At dusk, we set up lawn chairs in the backyard and lit citronella candles on the patio. When they arrived, my wife lit up in the way she only does when we have friends over.

"Looks like some druid ritual here," Greg said. He's not as smart as he thinks he is; he just watches the History Channel.

I nodded and popped open my first beer of the evening. I watched their son and daughter race our sons from one end of the yard to the other, smacking the stockade fence with a plastic baseball bat before wheeling around. Their son was fat and looked to be getting fatter. After five or six passes across the yard, he trundled over to the swing set and huffed and panted for at least a minute.

"Want some burgers?" I asked.

Nancy nodded and got up to tend to her son. I went to prepare the grill.

Once it was fully dark, Greg produced a flashlight and began to read off some sheets of paper, stuff he'd printed off the Internet.

"The star's called 'Alnilam,'" he said. The word gave him some trouble after that margarita. "It's the middle star in Orion's belt. It's the thirtieth brightest star in the sky." He glanced up. "Twenty-nine better watch his back."

"Can you see it?" I asked no one in particular.

"I think so," my wife said.

"It's too early," Greg said.

"Maybe it burned out already," my wife said.

"We'd know," Nancy said. "There are parties up and down the block."

The kids started a new game. Now that it was dark, they could start pretending. They wielded bats for swords and garbage pail lids for shields. "I'm Orion!" my younger son yelled.

"I'm Zeus!" Greg's son yelled.

My older son said, "More like 'moose.'" I laughed and Nancy shot me a look.

"David," I said, "that wasn't nice. Apologize."

He mumbled something, but I didn't press him to say more. Greg went to get the portable radio from his car. They were playing "Rocket Man," followed by "Ride Sally Ride." When the deejay came back on, my wife turned down the volume and pointed to the sky. You could see them now.

I sat and watched, even when the conversation lapsed and the three of them went inside to refresh their drinks and check the TV. I watched as the dark settled in thick and more and more stars appeared, seemingly all at once, like the music you sometimes don't hear playing during a movie until the violinist practically pokes you in the shoulder with his bow. It's right on top of you, and you feel a little embarrassed for not having noticed something that important.

I had a kind of communion with those stars.

Smog and haze lined the horizon like dirt along a windowsill, and the Parkway burbled like a river somewhere off in the distance. But those stars shone above us like they'd shone on the pyramids and the dinosaurs. They knew things; they'd seen. I swallowed more of my beer. My wife had never really loved me. I'd loved her once, but that had faded. It was the only time someone I'd loved had appeared to love me back, and so I was content to pretend. I could admit all this, under those stars. They understood. They knew how temporary things really were. After all, it wasn't even really them we saw, just some light they cast a long time ago.

I was by myself, near the shed. On the other side of the yard, my wife, Greg, Nancy and the kids were playing lawn darts. A cheer rose up; one of the kids must have made it into the ring. I stood by the grill and watched. One of the darts caught the light from the kitchen window and traced an arc like the sparklers we lit on the Fourth of July. It sunk into the ground with a thud.

My wife saw me. "Is it time?"

I checked my watch. "Almost." I had the boys turn out all the lights in the house and we blew out the candles. It was just after eleven. We stood on the patio and waited, radio off, necks craned up toward the sky. In the house just behind ours, a laugh track fizzed and subsided.

"When's it gonna happen?" my younger son said.

"Soon," my wife said, smoothing his hair.

"Who invented consolations?" Greg and Nancy's daughter said.

"'Constellations,'" Greg corrected.

"Yeah," the girl said. "Who invented them?"

Greg didn't say anything. He just looked up with the rest of us.

"Consolations are stupid," the girl said. "There's nothing there, it's just stars."

"It's like a connect-the-dots," Nancy said. "You need to draw lines between them."

And then, less than a minute later, as we were beginning to grow restless and even I was considering going inside to get another beer, it happened. It just winked out, like a dead bulb on a Christmas tree. Down the street, some people blew plastic horns left over from New Year's. In the paper the next morning we would read about a half-hearted attempt at a riot some drunk kids pulled in a strip mall. But none of us moved just then. We only stared up into that sudden nothing. I wanted to say something but couldn't.

Greg let out a long sigh and patted his stomach. "That's that," he said, and he went inside to go to the bathroom. Nancy went in, too, then my wife, then the kids. It was time to begin the rest of our lives.

Prompts

1. Create a story that focuses on a relationship in nature, then use it to examine a human relationship, as in "Cold Feet" and "Burning Out."

2. Start by choosing a place and then a mode of transportation. Write a story in which the transportation moves through a specific place and changes the character interactions. Examine the way this is accomplished in "Grid Lock" or "Welcome Wharf."

3. Notice the very different approaches to the same general subject used by "Cold Feet," "Feeding the Birds," and "Guide to Dissecting the First Bird of Spring." Choose one subject you are interested in writing about and approach it from three dissimilar angles.

4. Write something from the perspective of an

object in nature. Celebrate anthropomorphization as "Pathetic Fallacy" does.

5. Find a factoid about nature and write a story that incorporates that detail, as "Isn't That True?" uses the information about there being more fish than humans.

Characters

In flash fiction, there is no time to give lengthy back story about the characters, no space to provide the details of their furnishings or style of dress. "Show, don't tell" boils down to its most urgent base in flash writing. We need to know the characters through their actions in the story, and one or two well-placed details give us everything the author requires us to understand about the character. The pieces in this section exemplify dexterously drawn characters and their relationships with their families, friends, lovers, and strangers. The heart of good writing will always be characters portrayed with enough precision that they matter to the reader and have the complexity that makes the reader want to follow them. Each piece in this section is admirable for the way dynamic characters come alive, even through condensed writing.

Tattoos

John Paul Jaramillo

Little Neto announced to his folks, to his brother and the crew of fosters, he planned to dig his bicycle from the garage no matter the hour or night and ride over the Fourth Street Bridge to Union Avenue.

The *Jefita* was the only Ortiz to take the boy seriously. She argued, "Nothing but *desgraciados* downtown. Especially Union."

"That's where the men who ride the trains go for tattoos."

"Who told you that, Neto?" the woman asked.

"Tio Mitedio told me," Neto said.

"Ah, these men."

And when the boy was driven to the fields for work or to the landfill, Neto asked his *jefe* and the *jefe's compadre*, Julian, to show their forearms and shoulders. The boy traced at them with his little fingers.

"You like that ink, little Neto?" Julian said.

"Look at mines," the boy said rolling his flannel

sleeves and pointing out the nonexistent tatted designs on his scrawny arms.

The *jefe* never answered, never wanted to play along on those early morning rides out to side-jobs where the flat top ended.

"Oh, Neto. Look at those," Julian said. "They'll bring the women, no?"

"Don't get him thinking," the *jefe* said.

Maybe dragons and dinosaurs on his arms and his back, the boy decided. Great centipedes and crawling scorpions stretching to his legs. Bats or great screeching hawks wrapping the shoulders to his neck.

Neto studied the men's tattoos and concluded the eagle and the infantry insignia on each arm was the only evidence that his *jefe* ever existed outside of the house or the old neighborhood. He convinced himself that was what records your travels, the fact you were a man. To Neto and the other dark-haired and round-faced boys around Baystate and Box Elder Streets, around the unpaved and empty lots down by the highway where the boys ride bikes and wrestle and play their massive tournaments of marbles, tattoos were what made you *bien firme* and what proved you were a man. They all agreed.

And under the eaves of the garage and alongside the chicken cages was where the boys kept mason jars of spiders and water snakes, whatever they happened to capture in the fields or alleys. The glass so close the hens pecked and nearly knocked them over. At the end of long days Neto fed his *jefe's* animals and then chose one of his beasts.

"Neto!" the *jefita* cried.

"I want my tattoo like this spider," the boy demonstrated.

"Get your *animales* out of my kitchen. No place for that in my kitchen."

Once, Neto saw a man with hotrod flames on his shaved skull and neck working the bumper cars at the Huerfano County Fair, and immediately begged his mother. He envisioned inked fire demons on his neck and shoulders. In his coloring books he chose the colors and he chose the body parts, drawing and coloring in biceps and torsos with endless patterns of gore and depth.

The *jefita* gasped when she saw. "Get it out of your head, Neto," the *jefita* said. She held him in her wide arms like a baby and he struggled. "You're just a little thing." Finally, she relented and released the boy. Told him he would have to wait until far after her death and burial. And his father's death, and possibly the death of all his *Tios* and most of the *comadres*.

He reminded her of the *jefe's* tattoos, a bird and the word mother on his biceps along with his Army tats. He reminded her of the *compadre* Julian's and Mitedio's Marine tattoos on both of their forearms.

"Your *jefe* was old already," she argued. "In the Army when he got those. And your father's ink itches at him anyhows, Neto. And the *compadre* Julian is a damned fool. No woman would have him."

The boy asked, "What about Mitedio?"

"Ah. Your *tio*? Your *tio* was born with them."

One time, late at night, Neto disappeared into the bathroom with Tio Mitedio's pen knife. At first he just pretended to shave and scraped hair from his face. He got into the *jefe's* shaving cream and then his cologne. Then he drew and grated broad random arcs at his forearm until the tile and floor ran a river of the blood. It was an experimental gash, making the boy ache and wail for his Mama.

"There's a hell of a lot of blood here," the *jefita* warned as she ran over the boy's forearm with the *strapajo*. "He needs stitching."

"What the hell was he doing in here?"

"Your tattoos remember?" she said. "He can't get it out of his head and now look." She wiped at the boy's trembling tears. "It's okay, *mijo*."

"Oh Christ."

"No lie," the *jefita* said as she explained the expense to her husband. The doctor visit and the bill for stitches.

"Those doctors run a *pinche* racket, no?" the *jefe* said.

"Is that all you have to say to me?"

"What?"

"He cut himself nearly to death with that damn blade. What the hell was Mitedio thinking giving this to him?"

"He asked for it."

"*Oy lo*. Asked for it. Neto did you ask for this?" she said. And to this the boy nodded and giggled from his seat on the toilet.

The *jefe* said, "You're overreacting, *mujer*. A boy has to have some scars eventually, no?"

Last Cuts
Andy Bailey

Tom didn't say anything to his son the whole ride over, hadn't said anything since waking Jack up at 6:15, an hour earlier than most school days. Coach Coe put the list up at 7:00 and Jack wanted to be there right at 7:15; late enough so he'd miss the initial rush and early enough so he'd have time to deal with things before school started at 8:00. Jack said that, said "things" when they had made the plan the night before, and it seemed to Tom as good enough a word as any.

The low-flung outline of the junior high slouched in the gray domelit morning, scarlet streaks of light slinking up from the edge of the horizon like snake tracks. Only a handful of cars in the parking lot. Tom pulled the Camry around to the gym, where a trash can propped open a green door. He shifted into park and looked at Jack. "Will you come let me know? That okay?"

Three boys emerged from the gym, laughing

and walking with the pliant one-two rhythm and exaggerated hitch of athletes. Jack slumped down in his seat and watched them walk past, then slung his backpack over his shoulder and opened the door. "Guess I should, yeah." He kept his hands in his pockets as he shuffled inside, swallowed by the glare of the lights off the freshly-waxed court.

A man in a t-shirt, jeans, and cowboy boots leaned on the front hood of a large black truck across the lot, the cherry of his cigarette cutting through the morning haze as he wove it to his mouth and back. He looked from Tom to the door and back, his tired face hiding the anxiety his hands betrayed: shifting the cigarette back and forth, flicking invisible ashes, smoothing his goatee. Tom raised his hand off the wheel and waved. The man held his cigarette between his thumb and forefinger and jabbed it forward in response, like putting a period on the end of a sentence.

He'd decided he'd let Jack skip first period if he didn't make the team. Give him some time to regroup as he took him to breakfast at Shari's and tried to explain that what we withdraw doesn't always equal what we deposit. He'd keep his voice steady, looking Jack in the eye as he lied and said that twenty years from now this morning would be just another smoothed-over bulge on the melted clump of his youth. He'd tell of his own failures, of losing the junior class presidential election or getting rejected from his first choice fraternity, not so much to ease the sting as to commiserate in it.

But maybe he couldn't explain at all. Maybe silence was the best he could do, and he'd let the stale cherry pie rotating in the case and the smear of the waitress' pink lipstick remind Jack that sometimes life sucks and all we have is the ragged knowledge that tomorrow might suck or it might not.

A tall, gangly kid came out of the gym and didn't say anything as he walked past the smoking man and climbed into the passenger seat of the truck. The man remained motionless against the hood, gazing up toward the sky as he took a final puff on the cigarette and ground it against the truck's front bumper. He flicked the butt towards a trash can as he got in; it arced out and hit the edge, bouncing up and scraping against the side of the can as it plunked against the pavement. The truck's engine coughed twice then caught, trembling scream settling into a slow chug as it accelerated past.

Then Jack came out, eyes downward, walking briskly, fidgeting with the strap of his backpack. Something tight caught inside of Tom's lungs and he wheezed for breath. Jack approached the driver's side and Tom fumbled to roll the window down, Jack's breath leaving foggy ghostprints on the glass as it disappeared into the door. Cold air rushed in and Tom killed the motor and looked at his son. Then Jack nodded and Tom nodded back.

"Name was on the bottom of the list. It was Trent Edwards, then K.J. Fletcher, and it was all in alphabetical order so I thought I was out." Jack shifted up and back on the balls of his feet, his eyes darting from the steering wheel to the stereo knobs to the mug of cold coffee in the holder. "It was written in different color than the others, like he added me later or something."

"But you're on the team."

"I'm on the team." Tom smiled and so did Jack and then they both looked towards the gym door. "I'm going to hang here before school. Coach brought out some balls and a few of my teammates are shooting around." He said it easily, no hesitation or stutter. Teammates.

Tom imagined the scrawl of handwriting on the bottom of the list, *Jack Faller*, and wanted to see it himself. But he didn't want to embarrass Jack, and when his son broke into a run back towards the gym Tom wanted to get out and run with him, run past the parking lot and football fields and city and mountains beyond, run past his job and his two story home and his herniated disc and past the heaving mound of years that separated him from the burning blush of his own youth when his name scribbled on a page meant everything.

Instead, though, he started the car and headed to work.

In The Leaves
Emma Gilbert

He used to drink black tea, like an Englishman. At first, the concept struck you as deeply discordant with his character, his vibrant perpetual motion, the rush-rush-rush dynamism of him that seemed to scream coffee or nothing. At work, he threw back black-brewed battery acid like everyone else, wincing at the brutal strength of it and then grinning, as if to show he was man enough for anything that ever was poured into a forty-cup urn. At home, though, he drank tea, back in the black-and-white days before teabags, when everything had to be steeped and boiled and strained; when you had to debate such questions as *milk before, or milk after?* and *Oolong, my dear, or Darjeeling?*

It all seemed like a lot of deliberation for a man like Bill. You told him so, once, and he laughed and brushed it off, saying, "I *am* Canadian. You always forget that."

It was only after you kissed him that you understood what tea meant to Bill.

So many little things to draw together into the whole—kettle, tea leaves, teapot, teacups, strainer. You sat stiff-backed at his kitchen table, ankles crossed under your chair, and watched him padding to and fro, adjusting things, tending. You watched the curious angle of his shoulders slowly rectify itself as he worked. When, at length, he set the filled teapot down on the table, he raised his eyes to yours for the first time that afternoon, and they were bright and guileless, unflinching.

"I'm taking the girls to see the ball game on Saturday. You wanna come? Bring your gang and we'll make an afternoon of it."

It might have been any other afternoon. It might have been the previous week, or the previous month, or the month before that. Tea, you realised, was a ritual, for Bill, like gardening, or yoga. It absorbed him, calmed him; it took the fierceness of his feelings and muted them, siphoning them out like steam. You stared up at him, then, with the copper of your kiss still tart in the back of your throat, and he had put it aside, willfully forgotten it. It was all in the tea, now, steeping steadily on the table, waiting to be drunk. Or poured away.

You couldn't blame him. After all, you had made it fairly clear to him that it had been a mistake.

In those days, Bill drank his tea with six or seven sugar cubes, disgustingly sweet, so saccharine-thick it was barely liquid any longer. You drank yours black and bitter, and, forgetting, swallowed the dregs.

Not Like You, Not At All
Venita Blackburn

Not to be rude, but I was married to a man like you in my twenties. He was beautiful and we were jealous, jealous of everyone, we were kissing fish that suck and drown. We built a pretty cage for ourselves with bougainvillea entwined lattice and had sex a lot to keep from talking. Sometimes he spoke of joining the Army like his father, but he was lazy as fog and became too old. For nine years we had eye jittering sex four times a day. Then I married Eddie. He could make orange marmalade seem outright hilarious. Together we'd laugh anywhere like children in church. Strangers stared and smiled, but we couldn't stop. The cancer licked his skin bacon raw. When the ICU was full and his father folded in a chair, nephews at the foot of the bed, odd fuzzy ginger headed cousins from some nameless planet coughing in the doorway, and he lay pressed in the lasagna layers of hospital blankets he'd put my hand on his crotch. The laughter came wrung out against my will like sugar, like sweat, like a whole child, like oil from a grape seed, an unlikely miracle. I miss my Eddie. You don't look anything like him.

Readiness
Lee Reilly

The mother hugged herself into a question mark on the beach, wincing at the shriek of the lifeguard's whistle.

It was clear people didn't like being called out of the water. Little kids resisted. Grownups gestured, *Why?* The leggy lifeguard whistled and whistled while swimmers straggled out of the water as slowly as they could, and a teen flashed her the finger. Empty of swimmers, the lake lapped peacefully. On the beach, everyone, even the mother, wondered, *What next?*

"Go," the voice on the walkie-talkie said, and the pretty lifeguard walked into the lake, grabbing hands as she went, stray adults. Come with me, she said, All you have to do is walk. Reluctantly, barefoot recruits tossed their sunhats and sodas and followed her into the water.

And now they are 30 strong, hand in hand in hand, perpendicular to the beach, walking through water, heads bowed; a human chain of rescuers advancing toward another chain of rescuers, scanning, scanning, closing the space between them. They might be line dancers in a Texas bar or children learning the Virginia Reel. To the helicopter pilot hovering above, the two lines of rescuers advancing toward each other look like a religious ritual he once saw in a movie.

But they're accidental rescuers, elbow-deep in water and uncertainty. Silt swirls at their feet, and, looking down into murk, they wonder what can be seen in such conditions: a child's hand reaching? long hair floating?

But what should I do? an old man asks the man next to him, and he sends the question up the human chain, stranger to stranger, all the way to the lifeguard. *What should you do?* she thinks, impatient. Look, she thinks. Look and hope you're not the one who finds her, she thinks. But she can't say that to a volunteer: Look and try not to see a child in distress.

"Just look," is what she says.

Just look and pretend it's not happening to you, is what she thinks. And also (her thoughts swimming now, disobeying, diving deep): Look, and don't think about the message you left on his voicemail or what happens if the test is positive. What he'll say. What you'll do. Or how this happens—appearances, disappearances, any of it.

Now the loudest sound on the scene is the beat of helicopter blades—or is it a new heart inside her? Then, under the whoosh whoosh of the helicopter, the lifeguard hears the bleat of the mother's thoughts, which is impossible, isn't it?

This can't be. That's what the mother on the beach is thinking. This isn't happening to me. I won't let it. Maybe my girl's at home. Maybe her father took her.

Maybe I should never have been a mother.

Suddenly in the distance, the other chain of rescuers breaks, mid-water. Hands drop. People cluster. What's happening? The lifeguard can't see that far. Was the little girl found? At home? On a bus? In the water?

Her walkie-talkie crackles. A voice sounds.

But now the mothers hear nothing; they can't, they won't, it's not time yet.

Candy Cane
Shari Hack Jones

She was two lanes away from the curb waiting for the light to change. It was 5:00 on Thanksgiving, and she was heading home to an empty apartment. A Chinese take-out order was snugged safely in the back seat so she wouldn't snack on the way home. The usual homeless guys were on the corner, asking for handouts, the liquor store an easy block away. One man flashed her a peace sign. She responded with one of her own. The guy trotted over to her window.

"Here, you need this," he said, handing her a shrink-wrapped candy cane.

"Thanks," she said, smiling. All her life people had told her she didn't smile enough.

When they said that it made her feel like smiling even less. But, this time it was genuine.

The light was still red. The man dashed back to his post on the curb. She reached into her purse for a dollar. He was back at the window. She handed him the money.

"I don't want your money," he said. "I just want to go dancing with you!" She laughed as he repeated, "I just want to go dancing with you!" The light was green by now. No one was behind her as she lingered for one more moment, basking in a long forgotten feeling of what it felt like to be wanted.

Her Favorite Color
Christopher Duggan

1:43 p.m., July 17, 1987—Standing on a Saharan street corner in Soho, Sam could hear himself sweating. It ran in rivulets from his fingertips and splashed on the sidewalk. What he wanted was water—and Camille. They had agreed to meet at 1:00 p.m., but with New York traffic, she was not officially late yet, and she certainly wasn't sitting in a café somewhere, sipping a cool drink with friends, their date forgotten or never registered in the first place.

Sam's day: Up at 7:00 a.m., cornflakes, newspaper, shower, select blue shirt (because she had always said that was her favorite color), call to verify, no answer, probably left already, three transfers and a five-block walk to this corner, 57 minutes early, wait, semicircles of sweat from his armpits spreading across the expanse of the blue shirt, 1 p.m., no Camille, wait, wait, wait, wait.

There had been a water vendor two blocks ago, but if she showed up while he was gone, he would never know, and he would have no choice but to wait even longer, not leaving for anything until the heat overcame him—the New Yorkers stepping over his sun-baked body until the crows came and picked away his meager flesh through the rents in the blue shirt until that was all that was left, along with his bleached skull, until, just maybe, she would walk past and look down and think, "Blue is my favorite color."

So, he would stay—another 15 minutes, maybe 30, thirsting and hating himself for loving her.

She was coming.

He knew it.

Unable to Wrap Neat Packages
Myra King

My father drank all his life until there was no life left to drink. You could say he died of thirst.

My mother was dried up before she was thirty, but never craved the oblivion of drink, the muted haze of religion was her preserve. She God-bothered on Sundays while my father made his pilgrimage daily, to the local bars.

For us there was no kaleidoscope of a child's wonder to recall, only the drone of our parents' voices competing to win but never succeeding beyond the cataclysm of broken crockery, or dinner plates full of the unwanted, splattering the low glass ceiling of our existence. In this saints and sinners upbringing it was the silence we craved.

So now I enter my mother's kitchen and see the cup upturned on the sink, the teaspoon neatly by its side. Her last act, for the packet of aspirin sits beside it, buoyed up bulkily, wrapper peeled back, two shiny aluminum foil blisters popped and vacant. Pills drowned and downed at the onset of pain. Dissolvable.

I do not want to look too closely.

The air in here is lazy and I open the window, find it stuck halfway, laugh and curse as sash cords disintegrate into grey and flake to the floor. I see my feet shuffling their impatience, the boards bearing up under creaking complaints.

And then I realise this kitchen *is* my mother. From the curtains' patterned harshness to the dying flies buzzing their last dance on the windowsill. It is the shell of her life, like the newspaper turned to the finished crossword on the table, or the banana browning in the cracked white bowl I bought her for Mother's Day. And here is the script of her life, her bible, lying on the un-scrubbed sideboard with her name written in the beginning, claiming ownership in her eight-year-old's scrawl. There is dust on the cover.

I remember my mother was quiet the last few times I saw her.

My brother will be here soon and I will talk of a funeral and probate, although he will demur and say he doesn't want to think of these things yet, so can I deal with them, like I did our father's? His tears will beg their pleas. And he will say how I, his sister, am so much better at stuff like that. He will actually say 'stuff.' Never itemising the words. Never bringing them to name.

And he does, when I let him in, do just that.

I stand by the sink and look down at the cup, and before I can stop him, my brother has turned over the aspirin packet, taken the empty hidden other box crumpled beneath it and read the name, our mother's name, but this, as well, he does not bring to voice.

I glance over his shoulder, feel the drying of my palate, my tongue sticking to its reluctance to say what I also see is written on the box in tight pharmacy script, almost unpronounceable but as familiar as sleep, and I, too, hold the silence.

Stillman
Amy Braziller

He parks his truck every evening in the space that used to be his, left vacant every evening until midnight when he returns home, ready to sleep. He knows that by morning, the woman who doesn't own a car, who now lives in the apartment with the window that looks toward the 7-11, will lift the blinds with her left arm, hunch her body underneath the blinds, and look out, noticing that again, his truck is there.

It is this steadiness that holds Gabe Stillman to that parking spot, the one that used to be his when he lived in her apartment, when he thought he wanted a home. He needs to know that despite his readiness to be on the move at any moment, somebody is tracking him, marking his presence, a comfort felt for the nine years when somebody else declared his home. During those years, he could not go missing, because there would always exist someone to inform the authorities if he did not report when expected.

He existed because his absence would be noted.

It was actually a very pragmatic decision for Stillman to give up the apartment and choose his truck as home.

On Monday-Thursday evenings, Stillman pulls into the parking spot around midnight, tosses his backpack onto the passenger seat, and collapses on his homemade bed—a simple single mattress propped up on a two foot platform underneath his white camper shell. He usually sleeps in his underwear, green sweatpants, white cotton t-shirt, and a black watch cap, comforted by the sense of being fully clothed, a habit of most of his adult life, always ready if necessary. On Friday-Sunday evenings, he chooses the woods, a familiar terrain where he can march all day with a load of 75 pounds, armed with a Bowie knife and his memories, which often are enough to obliterate the silence, the stillness that reminds him that if he forgets to be alert, he might not be ready for his next move.

When he isn't in his truck or out in the woods, Stillman hides out at the local university, comfortable with a number, a photo, and a card that secures his passage into the building, into the shower, into a library that allows him to conceal the interminability of his days. Most days, he passes amongst hundreds without speaking to anybody, and when he on occasion finds himself desiring words, he only speaks of writers, especially poets like Kaminsky, telling anyone who listens how he would like to write the same poem over and over because like Kaminsky, he knows that to leave an empty page means surrender. For Stillman, surrender is never an option.

Tonight, when he returns at midnight to his parking spot, he tosses his backpack onto the passenger seat and collapses, knowing that the predictability of morning, the brief parting of the blinds by the woman, will silence any of his dreams that portend his need to move. In the morning, he exits the truck, walks to the 7-11 to take a piss and grab his coffee, and returns to the hood of his truck, where he will sit, awaiting the moment when she will lift the blinds.

Wanting
Brian Alan Ellis

It's late. And already you've listened to the same record eight times in a row; it's a sad record. And you've smoked too many cigarettes. And you've had one too many beers. And you've read too much poetry; you even tried writing one, but it wasn't very good. And you can't sleep. And the roommate's cat is still scratching at your bedroom door, wanting to be let in so it can piss all over your stuff… again. And you're scheduled at work in the morning, having just closed on your supposed night off. And the sinks at the restaurant are all backed up. And being that you are the dishwasher, they expect you to manage this during the busy season, the fuckers. And goddamn it if your woman still hasn't come back; she's probably gone for good. And right now you want something so bad.

So you make the slow death-walk to the convenience store down the street—an empty headed, skeleton-like walk—for you plan on foolishly picking up more beer and another pack of cigarettes. And your want follows you there, like a maddened crocodile burning you with its senseless bite. And you think about how you haven't been eating much lately. And you guess it's because you've been too disgusted to, though you still drink and smoke and, when offered, snort things up your nose.

That annoying buzzer goes off as you rattle into the store; you really wish they'd fix it.

And there is a man pacing the aisles wanting to know where the pickles are; he says to the clerk behind the counter, "Hey, where you keep all them pickles at?" And the clerk is too busy with other customers to tell the man where the pickles are kept. And because of this, the man becomes so agitated about not being able to have his pickles that he begins howling and throwing items across the store. And you notice the clerk reaching blindly for something behind the counter, possibly a gun; probably not a pickle. And you realize, then, that when a man's want for something is bad enough, regardless of whatever that something is, he will go to any number of extremes to get it. And so finally, as you are being rung up, the clerk tells the man, in so many expletives, where the pickles are kept—thus happily concluding your mini convenience-store epic for the night—and it makes you wish that other wants were as easily attainable.

Now, again in the silent torture of this dirty room—some cruel memory souring the walls, viciously, like wisps of a flaming hell—you cling to your purchases like a nun would her rosary beads.

And while Death waits to spoon us away to some place either better or worse than wherever it is we are now, what poor idiot could continue wanting something so seemingly simple as a good night's rest?

The Ambulance Driver
Nicholas Morris

The ambulance driver was new on the job. He'd spent months driving sweet little old ladies to dialysis appointments, all the while craving real action, the kind that saved lives and earned commendations from the mayor. His first lights-and-siren call came just after dusk from a bad part of town. Adrenaline pounded in his temples as cars pulled over and red lights turned green for his bus. The veteran chattered in code on the radio from the passenger seat, said "turn right here," then "left by the gas station."

The girl, no more than eight, wore a yellow sundress drenched in blood, a darker shade than the driver had ever seen. Her grandmother wailed, calling out to a god who paid no attention. Some of the bystanders tried to comfort her; others stared at the pavement or the sky. The ambulance driver lost his dinner in the sewer grate near the road, wiped his mouth, and wondered what he would tell his wife in the morning when she asked about his big day from the other side of the bed.

The veteran finished his cigarette before zipping up the bag.

Prompts

1. After reading "Tattoos," write a story about a character you have written about before, describing his or her first major scar.

2. Write a story fueled by a relationship in which a parent wants something very badly for their child, as in "Last Cuts."

3. Create a piece where one character makes another character reconsider her image of herself, as occurs in "Candy Cane."

4. As in "Wanting," write a piece that uses a second-person perspective to give us an intimate view of a character.

5. Write a piece like "The Ambulance Driver," in which you put a new employee in a challenging career field.

Sins, Secrets, Confessions and Obsessions

Flash fiction works as a perfect form for confessing secrets, both fictional and fictionalized. This section explores the shadows of lives, secrets not talked about, and things that exist but are left unsaid. Fast Forward has often published stories that experiment with the confessional as short story. Our fifth collection continues the exploration of sin and savior, confession and clemency, obsession and the secrets we all carry.

I Caught my Daughter's Hair on Fire Today
Jamey Trotter

It is my weekend with my daughter. It is Saturday. We have watched cartoons, we have eaten pancakes. Out my apartment window, there are other apartment buildings, and one thick long branch from the tree below. The tree is pointing up to the sky, one finger extended, "thank you jesus," a ballplayer who has just made a play. You can watch the branch from my couch.

Today there are no leaves on it.

Anna wants to go to the mall. During commercials, because otherwise she does not respond, I ask, "What do you want to do today, buddy?" Had she said, go to the beach, I would have packed our suits and driven the 1500 miles. Had she said, ride a horse, I would've gone to U-Haul to rent a truck with which to steal a horse.

She shrugs. I suggest, "Movies? Zoo? Bunny hill at Loveland? Kitty room at the animal shelter? Playground in Golden?" These are all things that made her happy not long ago.

The cartoon is back on. I settle into my lounger, stare at the branch. The cartoons are weirder now. This one seems Japanese but I am not sure why. I guess it is the characters' eyes, large and innocent.

She says, "Mall," so softly that I have to look over to the couch to see that she is looking for my reaction. I hate the fucking mall. I would rather go to the dermatologist to have sex sores frozen and shaven off.

"Maybe we should steal a horse instead?" I suggest.

The branch taps on the window, like a ghost, like the reaper. It must be windy. She repeats, "Mall."

We get ready for the mall. She takes a shower by herself, now. After I turn the water on just right, I must leave. So when she calls "DA-DEE" from behind the closed door, I rush in. "Will you dry my hair?" she asks as she towels off.

"Of course, baby," I choke. She has brought a hairdryer, the one her mother used for those few years, the loud incessant noise that seems as if it will never end, that gets in the crevasses of the ear canal like a bee has flown in, that whirrrrrs like the margarita blender to the American tourist in Mexico who has just hiked an old pyramid ruin and barely made it down and then refuses water on the bus because he knows what will happen when he drinks the water and then he waits, wafts in the wail of the blender at the bar with the other tourists, getting served dead last because he is ugliest.

The sound of the hairdryer still annoys me; waiting fifteen minutes for a shitty drink on my honeymoon did too.

But I am happily gripping the machine in my left hand and brushing with the other. Her hair has gotten long. It is thick and silky and black, homemade noodles dipped in molasses. She sits in the sink wrapped in her towel. Though much has changed, this routine has not, except her mom used to dry and brush while I busied myself with gathering for whatever impending outing: water in Nalgene, milk in sippy cup, orange pretzels for snack, box of raisins, coats, gloves, sunglasses.

FOOMP her hair is aflame. "DADDY!" she says.

"FUCK!" I say. The flames started at mid-hair, about at her shoulders, and already the bottom half has fallen to the ground. The smell of burning hair is disgusting and I want to puke.

I panic, I am blowing on the flames like a birthday cake. I make a wish. I slip on the hair on the linoleum and fall hard. My tailbone. This one time as a kid, I fell off the side of a hill while chasing a soccer ball and landed on my tailbone and couldn't walk for a week.

I cling to the sink and pull myself up to find the flames around her ears now. She is shrieking and sobbing and hitting herself in the head.

"Why Daddy?" she pleads above the sound of the hairdryer and burning hair. In the mirror, she looks into my eyes. "Why did you cheap on Mommy? Why are you the bastard and had to leave?" Her face is so contorted. It reminds me of *The Scream*.

I huff and puff to blow the flames down. I turn the faucet on. I am using handfuls of water to douse the flames. We both see it working so we smile at each other, a sobbing sort of smile—things will be okay. We are Rwanda refugees saved by the UN, we are New Orleans residents saved by FEMA.

"I'm sorry," I whisper.

The hairdryer falls into the sink, by her feet. It clanks, a quarter-second passes for me to lament it being on still.

There is a hiss, the sound of a zitzit.

She convulses. I grab her. I am going to throw her. My arms burn. My body burns it singes it stings it is exhilarating excruciating frightening ending.

Pop! The lights are out. We are on the ground, the dirty fake tile, panting like lovers, mewing like kittens.

In the next room, the tree branches screech on the window.

Covet the Compulsion
Richard Hartwell

He is waiting in what passes for the passenger lounge in the Coos Bay-North Bend Airport, waiting to catch a local prop flight to San Francisco and a return to the girl who had called to say she was late. Yeah, late. Yeah, missed. You know… It! He thinks he must return to do what's right. So many times he's tried to do what's right, after doing what's wrong. The friend of a friend who gave him a lift to the airport waits as well. The friend of the friend got laid off from the mill last night at the end of his shift and the two of them are nursing a couple of beers. The friend of the friend is wearing a black Stetson and a clean jean jacket, dirty jeans and steel-toed work boots. He is older than the one trying to be right and to that one the friend of the friend looks so right with the linked band of matched turquoise stones set in the silver band wrapped around the Stetson.

Even while listening to the friend of the friend bitch about being laid off, the one waiting for the flight kept thinking that the hat looked cool. He wants a hat like that. He really should have a hat like that. He feels he really needs a hat like that.

In his mind the waiter for the plane pictures the look on the girl's face as she meets him in the airport in San Francisco when he gets off the plane, to do the right thing for being wrong. In his mind he's wearing a black Stetson with a silver band inset with turquoise. He needs that hat, that new persona, in order to embrace the rights ahead and leave the wrongs behind. He suggests to the wearer of the hat that this will be just right for the girl on her way to the airport in San Francisco to meet the boy that is usually wrong. So right that they, the seeker of the hat and its current owner, walk the half block down from the airport parking lot to the state liquor store and buy a bottle of the good stuff. It is agreed. The coveter of the hat pays for the pint that the two of them start to share out of the brown bag in the alley behind the state liquor store and the laundry.

Somewhere between the alley in North Bend and the airport in San Francisco, worrying about the late girl becomes wrong and a few drinks become right. The Stetson becomes a need and no longer merely a want. So for the boy who for so many times has tried to do what's right after doing what's wrong decides to try it the other way around. He also tries the hat. The hat is too big. The turquoise stones are hazed glass. The silver band is plate. The girl isn't late, even to the airport.

How Temperance Made a Decision
Evon Davis

She leaned back from the window, an oily stain left on the glass where she had pressed her forehead for the past five minutes, wondering whether or not she had the courage to fling open the small-paned wings and throw herself to the hard concrete below. Oh, but what a horrific sight that would be for the passers-by. Was it really fair to them to have to witness her misery, to have it seared into their brains like a hot, bloody branding iron? And what about the poor people who would have to clean it up? How could they possibly swallow their bites of fish pie as they sat around the table, telling their children what a lovely day they had, remembering the caved-in side of her face that had taken the full impact?

Stepping away from the window, she thought, "Maybe not today."

Knackers
Mark Fallon

In the summer of my seventh year, when I had taken my First Holy Communion and was grown enough to wear my brother's hand-me-down slacks without having to roll the bottoms, a caravan appeared overnight at the crossroads about a mile out of our town. It wasn't like the bouncy tired aluminum-framed caravan my uncle lent us for a week each summer, and which huddled among scores of others in a sloping field that gave way to the black Atlantic. This one had big wagon wheels like in the Cowboys and Indians films my father brought me to when he was in the right mood, and they were rimmed with bands of shiny copper. The wagon had a cylindrical body that looked like someone had taken the fattest tree in the world, hollowed it, cut it into sections then moved themselves and everything they owned inside and taken to the road. It was the morning my father drove me from the hospital where I had spent the night after my most recent asthma attack, brought on by a game of football in the fields behind our town, and which had been forbidden by my mother. She sat next to my father, her stony face reflected in the rearview mirror. "That's enough from you," she said when I asked about the caravan, and she nudged my father who straightened and flexed his fingers on the steering wheel, mumbled something resembling agreement. I watched as we drove away. A blinkered mare with bony flanks was hitched in front, and before the wonderful caravan was swallowed by a bend in the road I spotted, in the shade next to her, a young stallion tethered by rope and chain to the tree branches above.

My parents owned a store on Main Street and we lived above it in four rooms: a kitchen and living room and two pokey bedrooms that looked over the hills toward the sea. Sometimes I could taste the salt in the wind in the early summer mornings. I shared the room with my grandmother who smelled of piss and spent her time worrying a rosary through her twisted claws. My brother Dan was in Dublin training for the priesthood. In the shop below mother weighed spuds, or carrots, or cabbage in the large silver scales that took up one end of the counter while father sat in the office taking stock with beautiful penmanship in a big black ledger. I would stand in doorways, or behind doorways, out of sight but within earshot, and in this way could hear what passed for conversation in the shop. It didn't take long for news of the caravan to spread.

"We should set the guards on them," said Mrs. Murphy as she twirled the corners on a sack of sugar.

"I hear they eat horsemeat," said Mrs. Flaherty.

"Of one thing I'm certain," said my father,

sticking his head around the corner of the office, "I'll be padlocking the door from now on."

When curiosity overcame my doghouse status and I asked again I was told only to stay away, that I would get the belt if I was caught up at the crossroads. It didn't seem fair.

"Get me my teef," granny hissed when I asked her.

She told me of gypsies, which she also called knackers, who were wild creatures older than the hills, made of nettles and barbed wire and darkness, and who crept, hungry, from their caravans in the night to hunt for little boys who hadn't said their prayers. "And what would they do with them?" I asked huffing on my inhaler.

"Boil them in a big black pot," she cackled, "and suck the marrow from their bones."

For two days I stuck to the house clutching my communion prayer book and rosary and hugging the walls. I prayed to Jesus to keep me safe from the knackers, but could not forget the caravan. I seemed to remember a friendly yellow curtain drawn across the windowed door.

On the third morning, having lain most of the night listening to the dark lump in the other bed snore and rattle, I dressed silently, and, armed with prayer book, rosary, and inhaler, crept downstairs and lifted the latch on the back door.

I made my way up the road out of town, cowslips nodding dew against my arm and cows hunkered down in the wet fields on either side. I tried to feel brave like Saint Patrick who stood up to the four kings of Ireland, but mostly I felt terrified even as I remembered granny's warning that knackers only come out at night. I jiggled the rosary in my pocket and offered a prayer to Jesus who my teacher, Father Joseph, responded was made of love and light when I asked why he couldn't be seen. Father Joseph also kept a bottle in his desk that he told me was filled with holy water that only priests can drink, and when I thought of this it made me glad for my brother Dan up in Dublin, made me strong, careful in my sandals, as I rounded the bend that led to the crossroads, to avoid the underfoot crunch of gravel that would signal my approach.

The yellow curtain I remembered seeing was not there. Neither was the boney mare. The open door gaped like a mouth swallowing the darkness inside. From in front of the caravan a feather of smoke coiled into the arched branches of trees that seemed silently to watch, and there was a sound like bubbling, and a faint humming, and a word or two in a language that was at once familiar and strange, and that spoke of sweet hay and wanderlust, and the coldness of stone. I felt the weight pressing down on my chest and although I reached again for my inhaler I didn't huff, glad enough of the familiarity of pain to be rooted to the road, my feet inching forward in baby steps.

Voyeur
Terry Persun

The next person slipped into the confessional and kneeled down. The Priest heard some scuffling, some wiggling. The kneeler squeaked. The Priest daydreamed as he spoke the familiar words. He waited.

"Father, I have sinned."

Not again? But, of course, this is how it went. This was the job. And so day after day, like the monotony of television, he listened, he thought, and he excused the sins of others as though he actually could.

Then a parishioner told him something amazing: That in order to enjoy your work, you must find what is exciting in the work. It was an innocent comment made in a small group setting.

And after several weeks, the Priest began to listen more closely while he sat on his side of the confessional. He found that the most outrageous and exciting things were happening all around him. People were ingenious in their adulteries, diligent in their crimes against one another. He listened as though it was his life they talked about, as if he were living in sin and pain and madness. And he grew to enjoy the madness, but, alas, it was all secondary.

So, he went into the streets and began to listen, to try to be a part of one of those stories. He walked down dark alleys waiting, just waiting for something to happen to him. But nothing did. Repeatedly, he would reach out and brush the breast of a woman walking past him as she left the church. He held matches until they burned his fingertips. He called people on the telephone and breathed into the receiver.

One day, he bought a gun. He didn't know what to do with it, but he could guess. He carried it, hidden, for days. Once he pulled it out—it was dark—and aimed it at someone walking by. It excited him. The coldness of the barrel. The gunpowder odor. He placed the barrel in his mouth and tasted metal, salty and acidic. He frightened himself with the thought of pulling the trigger.

Before he knew it, his madness pushed his mind into new shadowy places inside, places he couldn't explain. But, he was a man of the Lord and got a grip on himself. He entered the confessional one day, waited for the Pastor's familiar words, then said,

"Father, I have sinned."

He heard the Pastor take a deep breath and let the air out slowly. "I know," the man said. "I have been watching you."

Purpose
Amber Gordon

I have a tendency to reject things. This pushing away, I have discovered, is the very mechanism for my survival. Or a long path of self accepted and moderated suicide – for what is death but a separation from those we know? So in my unfolding of days I have come to terms with the idea of rejecting but not rejection. That must be what keeps me human.

I am waiting for him. I've seen him countless times in my sleep—during what I call contact moments—because they are more than silly glimpses into the conscious, sub-conscious, unconscious rat trap of barriers that can never be breached by the waking. I do have regular dreams—confusing moments in my sleep which I can typically trace back to a bit of conversation I overheard in the day, a commercial I saw hours later and the emotional reaction to the smell of whatever food I've moved by since my last "sleep." It is the contact moments that are valuable—not the dreams—because the contact tells me where to go, what to say, who to watch.

Some say my kind is not mythic. And I would wager that they are right. But not because we are not of mythic quality but because the world has lost touch with what the word means. Immortal (that is always a key term) but it is translated incorrectly, we should be called the undying. The progression towards death can never be rejoiced in and is always rejected. You can never know what it feels like to be in this constant state of longing to return to those we know without the ability. So the world rejects me.

"One cannot live without…" I heard him before he rounded the corner—it wasn't the voice I recognized it was the way it matched the skin of his hand. Veined and cruel.

"It really is an extraordinary day… no car." His bowler hat neatly hid his quick glance each way as he stepped from the curb and headed for the news stand where I had been looking at the latest lines of the world. The smell of smoke and ashes preceded him falling from his shoulders and rippling away like the perpetual invader.

"Yes, perhaps in the presence of guardian angels," he said happily. I had seen this part already. He put his cell phone back in his right pocket and that was all the confirmation I needed. His stride quickened and his footsteps rang out rigorous and dull on the concrete. The deep moaning push of worms startling into a reactionary state of burrowing followed beneath him —a deep hum not unlike the undesired lawn activities of the Saturday 6:00 a.m. neighbor we all know.

"Sister." His nod of approval and recognition made me smile slightly—control my excitement—and I nodded in return holding his gaze.

My tongue moved to a traditional greeting, "*Dio vi benedica. Buongiorno a voi, padre.*"

"Ah you speak beautifully. *Che Dio la grazia il vostro cammino.*" Yes, grace my path. For breakfast he had eaten pastries made with the wrong type of flour, perhaps a very dense muffin or a scone, and coffee—very bitter coffee with cream.

Contact had taken three days on living time and weeks to build during my sleep. Purpose was unknown. Sometimes knowing the purpose just got in the way of completing the task. Or it completely redirected the task or the outcome of the task. To push my contact moments had always turned out to be a play in the changing of fate and there were times where it had turned out badly. I would be satisfied with knowing who he is.

He stood feet away, absently sniffing his fingers as he glanced quickly over the available pages of fodder, picked up a newspaper, and threw down his coins.

"Thank you, Father. Very kind."

He raised his hand to the vendor and said nothing, rejecting any conversational niceties. And so, I would grace him with my path.

Greetings from Tel Aviv

Jonathan Danielson

During the split second the bus exploded as it pulled away from the central station, Jason didn't linger on whether or not he would first burn from the sticks of dynamite or C4 or plastique or whatever that was strapped to the screaming man three rows up, or if he would simply explode, if the blast would be so great his body wouldn't feel anything when it broke him apart on a molecular level, but rather he thought more about how his parents were going to be *soooo* pissed when they heard word from his organizer in his thick Israeli accent that their son had wandered away from the group and was where he shouldn't have been, and that's why he was on a bus that exploded as it pulled away from the central station, because he went to hang out with this girl he met from Ashod who wanted to show him the fortress and the shops and the tide and hopefully, Jason hoped, give him a BJ or at least a handy, but his parents wouldn't be angry at him for that, *high five* his Dad would've said, as instead they would be *soooo* pissed because they had thought this whole Birthright thing was a bunch of bullshit to begin with, considering he was born Catholic, raised agnostic, and the only Jewish blood in him, supposedly, was from a great-great-great-Grandmother on his father's side, who had died in Pittsburgh after giving birth to Jason's great-great-Grandfather, and who no one had ever spoken of because no one knew anything about her until Jason started digging around Ancestory.com during Christmas Break of his senior year, searching for anything Jewish, all so he could apply to go to Israel on Israel's dime, what with his parent's being too cheap, he said, to send him to Europe with the rest of the seniors in upper-level French, and what was the point of taking four years of French if he couldn't go to France, so the only way Jason figured he was getting out of the country was if someone else would spot the bill and the Jews would, Jason told his parents when he informed them of his Jewish heritage, *because we're the chosen people*, he tried saying with a straight face, and so he dumped French, which sucked because he sat next to Amy Scott, which was pretty awesome classroom real-estate and like his real-estate agent father always said, *location location location*, but on the plus side, since fourth-year French was an elective, he had one less class during the day and could come home and smoke out an extra hour before his parents came home from work and, he thought, he could use the extra time studying Hebrew, which, he figured, would help him once out of college when he wanted to be a lawyer or screenwriter or whatever, and he didn't realize what a dick he was being saying that to everyone until Allonia, this girl from Ft. Lauderdale with huge jugs, told him *you're a dick* when they were leaning against a balcony overlooking Haifa, when he was laying it hard for a BJ or at least a handy, and their guard, this other girl who looked younger than both of them even though she was carrying a loaded M1 Carbine, gave him a dirty look the rest of the time, and he couldn't figure out what the big deal was, why everyone was so serious and getting so upset about things, but then he didn't think about it, because then he didn't burn. He simply exploded.

Not Stealing Raymond Carver
John Kuebler

Lydia picks up Jack on the 101 outside Salinas. She can take him as far as Santa Barbara. She's driving back from the city and she could use the company.

He has impressed upon her a sort of Midwestern trustworthiness so that when they arrive in Santa Barbara, she invites him into her house, feeds him black beans and sliced avocados (from her own trees!—this is California, Jack thinks), and offers him the guest bed for the night.

She brings fresh towels and sees him studying the bookshelves. She pulls down a slim chapbook containing a strange story about house-sitting by Raymond Carver and she says that if he loves literature, he must read Carver. She recommends also Dostoevsky and Chekov and pretty much all the Russians, she says, and David Foster Wallace too. She implores Jack to make himself at home and wishes him goodnight, and if Lydia wants anything from him in return for her kindness, she never lets on she does.

In the morning Jack slips the chapbook inside his pack. It is a signed and numbered copy and is probably worth something. Lydia has been so trusting though, driving him 200 miles and opening her home to him, so he leaves the Carver and steals a Dostoevsky instead. The Dostoevsky is only a beat up old paperback and if he were to ask for it, he is certain Lydia would give him the book, gladly. But after she has been so generous, he can't bring himself to ask her for anything more.

He strikes out again upon the 101, carrying the Dostoevsky with him as a reminder of a stranger's kindness. He can't ever get through it though. All those complicated Russian names.

Three Things I Never Did after that Summer
Shelby Yaffe

I was drunk, drunk on life, drunk on life and bad mojitos, and I was sitting on a cobblestone corner in a beautiful square in a beach town in Italy when the monsters found me. They must have been lured by my platinum blonde hair, a rare shade in those parts. There were at least fifteen of them. Some were only children. They passed me around, touching what wasn't theirs, as I stayed silent in total fear. They abandoned me in the pebbles on the beach, me, alone with my numbness and tears.

There are three things I never did after that summer: I never went back to Italy, I never dyed my hair that Marilyn Monroe white, and I never again drank a mojito.

Prompts

1. As in "Voyeur," write a story about someone watching another character commit a sin.

2. Create a super hero with an obscure super power and put them in a situation where they interact with another character you have written about before. Use "Purpose," as a model.

3. After reading "How Temperance Made a Decision," write a scene in which a character fantasizes about something they will not follow through on.

4. Write about a character who is obsessed with a material object, as in "Covet the Compulsion."

5. Use the seven deadly sins (lust, gluttony, sloth, wrath, envy, pride, vanity) to create a list of capital sins you or a character has committed. Write a sentence about each one. Individually, you can choose to expand one of the lines into a story. Working in a group, you can exchange the sins, using other's confessions as the opening line for a new story.

Index

Index

Bailey, Andy	"Last Cuts"	116-119
Black, Lucy	"Grid-Lock"	97-99
Blackburn, Venita	"Not Like You, Not At All"	122
Blomstrom, Rachel	"The End"	3
Braziller, Amy	"Stillman"	133-135
Busheff, Nick	"First Date"	9
Cebula, Travis	"Sometimes the Only Response is Silence"	4
Corman-Roberts, Paul	"What's Strange"	39-40
Danielson, Jonathan	"Greetings from Tel Aviv"	157-159
Davis, Evon	"How Temperance Made a Decision"	147
Duggan, Christopher	"Her Favorite Color"	128-129
Ellis, Brian Alan	"Wanting"	136-137
Fallon, Mark	"Knackers"	148-151
Gates, Roberta Hartling	"A Trip to the Store"	71-74
Gordon, Amber	"Purpose"	154-156
Gilbert, Emma	"In the Leaves"	120-121
Hartwell, Richard	"Covet the Compulsion"	145-146
Hawke, Robin	"The Bride"	1
Hetzel, Drew	"The Monstrosity"	16
Hofbauer, Adam	"Touchdown Jesus"	54-55

Index

Jansing, Bryan	"Cold Feet"	86-88
Jaramillo, John Paul	"Tattoos"	112-115
Jones, Shari Hack	"Candy Cane"	126-127
Jordon, Nate	"The Rod of Correction"	68-70
Kearnes, Thomas	"Imitation of Life"	7
Kilkelly, Dan	"Two Full Minutes"	8
King, Myra	"Unable to Wrap Neat Packages"	130-132
Kuebler, John	"Not Stealing Raymond Carver"	160-161
Kuntz, Len	"What We Bury, What We Don't"	5-6
Laemmlen, Donna	"Centerville"	100-102
Larsen, Sonja	"Isn't That True"	95-96
Lewis, Susan	"Pathetic Fallacy"	94
Linforth, Christopher	"The Syndicate"	12-15
Milbrodt, Teresa	"Inherited Tastes"	19-21
Morris, Kona	"I'm Pretty Sure Nicolas Cage…"	46-48
Morris, Nicholas	"The Ambulance Driver"	138
Moloney, Bede	"On the Experience of Rain"	33-36
Olsen, Jon	"Ball, Shark, Pool, and C-3P0"	60-61
O'Rourke, Bernard	"The Last Velociraptor"	37-38
Persun, Terry	"Voyeur"	152-153

Index

Purdy, Matthew	"Burning Out"	105-108
Ransick, Chris	"Three Visitors"	27-30
Reece, Phil	"The Final Frontier"	52-53
Reilly, Lee	"Readiness"	123-125
Siskonen, Sacha	"Distillation"	65-67
Springsteen, Jennifer	"Welcome Wharf"	89-91
Stohlman, Nancy	"The Detritus"	41-42
Touhy, Andrew	"Acts of Faith"	22-23
Townsley, S.C.	"Somnium of Posterus Somnium"	24-26
Trotter, Jamey	"I Caught my Daughter's Hair on Fire…"	141-144
Tuite, Meg	"Virgin Debacle"	56-59
Traverse, Maureen	"My Life With Animals"	2
Vallières JP	"Tent"	79-82
Vaughan, Robert	"In it to Win"	49-51
Virgil, Erin	"Last of the Three Ravens"	31-32
Williams, John Sibley	"Guide to Dissecting the First Bird…"	92-93
Winograd, Kathryn	"45-Year Rain"	77-78
Wright, Kirby	"Feeding the Birds"	103-104
Yaffe, Shelby	"Three Things I Never Did after that…"	162
Zaikowski, Carolyn	"He Broke Pictures"	75-76

FF>> Press

is

*Leah Rogin-Roper, Kona Morris, Nancy Stohlman,
K. Scott Forman, Stacy Walsh
and Michael D'Alessandro*

This book is set in **Impact**, *Calibri and* Garamond
*typefaces. It was designed in Portland, OR and Denver, CO
and printed in Minneapolis, MN*